CAST OF CHARACTERS

FAMILY
SECRETS

*Five extraordinary siblings. One dangerous past.
Unlimited potential.*

Eric Jones—Accused of masterminding the World Bank heist, he must ask for help from the last woman on earth who wants to see him.

Leigh Montgomery—The crackerjack defense attorney couldn't refuse Eric's case, but would she tell him the truth about his secret child?

Jake Ingram—One of the Extraordinary Five genetically engineered siblings, the financial whiz suspects the Coalition set up his college pal, Eric, to get to him. The people he loves are no longer safe....

About the Author

JENNA MILLS

is a firm believer in the transforming power of love. A librarian's daughter, she's long been enthralled by stories of men and women who overcome great obstacles to be together. She was thrilled to be invited to participate in the FAMILY SECRETS project alongside many talented authors she's admired for years.

"Eric Jones and Leigh Montgomery stole my heart from the start," she says of *A Verdict of Love*. "Once they'd been the best of friends, but tragedy and a painful secret ripped them apart. Now, Eric turns to Leigh in the hour of his greatest need, and she knows she can't turn him down, even though letting him back into her life is sure to break her heart all over again."

When not writing romantic stories of suspense, Jenna spends her time with her husband and menagerie of cats and dogs in their Dallas, Texas, home. She loves to hear from readers (writejennamills@aol.com) and invites you to visit her Web site at www.jennamills.com.

A VERDICT
OF LOVE

JENNA
MILLS

Silhouette Books

Published by Silhouette Books
America's Publisher of Contemporary Romance

Special thanks and acknowledgment are given
to Jenna Mills for her contribution
to the FAMILY SECRETS series.

 SILHOUETTE BOOKS

ISBN 0-373-61373-3

A VERDICT OF LOVE

Visit us at www.silhouettefamilysecrets.com

Printed in U.S.A.

FAMILY SECRETS

Henry Bloomfield (d.) m. Violet Vaughn 2nd m. Dale Hobson

Susannah Hobson

Extraordinary Five

Connor Quinn (d.)

Jake Ingram

Ingram Family

Clayton Ingram m. Carolyn Cook

Zach Ingram
m.
Maisy Dalton

Gretchen Wagner m. Kurt Miller

Marcus Evans m. Samantha Barnes

Faith Martin

Gideon Faulkner

"Uncle" Oliver Grimble m. "Aunt" Agnes Payne

Evans Family

Russell (Russ) Evans
m.
Lynn Van Allen

Charles Evans
m.
Sarah Alexander

Seth Evans

Drew Evans

Laura Evans

Honey Evans

Holt Evans

—— Birth Family
---- Adoptive Family
m. Married
d. Deceased

For Frank and Timothy, police sergeant and
attorney-at-law, for endless patience explaining
the ins and outs of the legal system.
The mistakes are all mine.

And for Abigail.
Our summer together, when this story
came to life, will always own a precious,
magical place in my heart, as will you.
'Til we meet again...

Prologue

He kissed her goodbye with the first rays of the sun. She sighed softly and shifted, nestled deeper into the thick down comforter. Long, dark hair fanned out on the wrinkled white pillowcase where her head rested, and with a hand tucked under her chin, a soft smile curved her lips. The rhythm of her breathing was deep and even.

She was his best friend.

Or at least she had been.

Eric Jones turned abruptly and crossed to the small window overlooking Lake Michigan. A chill radiated from the glass, but the numbness seeping through him muted the bite. In the space of one single heartbeat, his life had changed in ways that could never be repaired.

His father was dead, killed in a freak accident.

And in his blind grief, in that hazy place of suspended reality, Eric had turned to his friend for comfort. Sweet, loyal Leigh. He'd accepted her embrace, demanded more. When she'd murmured words of comfort, he'd sought her mouth with his, driven by an unquenchable need to drink in all she had to give. And when driving need replaced bottomless sorrow, rather than having the good sense to put a stop to the craziness, he'd picked her up and carried her to his bed, eased her out of her jeans and sweatshirt, savored the feel of her warm nakedness, betrayed a sacred trust.

They could never go back to before.

His throat tightened, and the grief came crashing back, hard, violent, much like the freak car accident that had killed his father. Black ice. Christ. He still couldn't comprehend why his dad had been on the roads. Neither he nor Leigh had understood what his mother had been trying to tell them. He'd barely recognized her voice. Susan Jones had always been strong and stable, unshakable. But last night her voice had been broken, incoherent, her words nonsensical. Something about black ice and an eighteen-wheeler. His father. Police and ambulances. A hospital a few hours from Cloverdale. Dead on arrival.

Leigh had picked up the phone when it fell from Eric's fingers and gently spoken to his mother, then a police officer. And it was Leigh who'd explained it all to Eric, Leigh who'd called the airport, Leigh who'd gathered his friends.

Leigh who'd brought him comfort for a few mindless hours.

He needed to get home to Indiana. He needed to be there for his mother. She had no one else. Last night the blizzard that hit the midwest had shut down the roads and the airports, but this morning the winter wonderland beyond gave no hint of the devastation from the night before.

There should be some evidence, he thought raggedly, some remnant or trace. Pristine beauty shouldn't be possible when everything inside him sliced like shards of broken glass. But the community beyond his University of Chicago apartment sprawled like a quaint still-life. A fresh carpet of snow covered sidewalks and streets and rooflines, with trees standing so still, piles of white concealing their naked branches. Only a few stray flakes drifted through the hazy sunlight of early morning. Against the blue sky, a V of geese flew high and fast, as though they realized how late they were for their trek south.

The sense of loss cut sharp and deep, clear to the bone.

"Eric?"

He stiffened at the sound of her sleep-roughened voice, the feel of her soft hand settling against the leather of the jacket he'd already pulled on. His heart started to pound. He knew he needed to turn to her, to somehow make things right, but for the life of him, he had no idea how.

Never before had he made love to one of his best friends.

With cold certainty, he now realized Leigh shouldn't have been the one to stay with him. Matt and Ethan and Jake had all volunteered. They'd arrived within minutes of Leigh calling them, had stayed until well after midnight. He should have listened to them, let them stay, sent Leigh back to her dorm.

But damn, it was Leigh he'd wanted there with him.

"Go back to bed," he said, easing around to face her.

Nothing prepared him. Nothing prepared him to see her standing only a few inches away, the sheet wrapped around her tall, willowy frame, the early-morning light playing softly against her face. Concern glowed in her gentle brown eyes.

The sight hit like a punch to the gut.

"There's no need for you to be up," he said with a soft smile. Over the year they'd known each other, Leigh Montgomery had made it perfectly clear she was *not* a morning person.

She lifted a hand to his face. "Are you okay?"

Was he okay? Christ. He'd taken advantage of her trust and betrayed her friendship, crushed something rare and special, and *she* wanted to know if *he* was okay. "I need to get going."

The light in her eyes dimmed. "I'll go with you."

"No."

"Eric—"

"Don't, Leigh, okay?" He bit the words out more roughly than he'd intended, and when he saw the hurt wash across her face, he tried to gentle his tone. "I'm sorry. I'm so damn sorry. I just...need to get home."

Moisture glistened in her eyes. "Of course you do."

He tore away from her, grabbed his wallet and stuffed it into the back pocket of his jeans. "You can...stay as long as you like. Just lock up on your way out." He grabbed his keys and strode toward the door, but couldn't make himself walk out on her, not after last night.

"Leigh," he said, turning toward her. She still stood exactly where he'd left her by the window, one hand clutched around the ends of the sheet, watching him through big bruised eyes. Long dark hair tangled around her bare shoulders.

"I'm sorry," he said, and meant the words more deeply than she could ever know.

Finally she moved. She lifted her chin and crossed to him, walked with that leggy grace she had down to an art form. Only when she stood so close he could feel the heat from her body did she speak. "I'm not."

The words were soft, damning. "Leigh—"

"There were two of us here last night," she reminded, again lifting a hand to his face. "I wanted to be there for you."

That was what he was afraid of. Compassion and loyalty had driven her to give him a gift he couldn't accept, one that shattered the careful boundaries they'd established.

"I don't deserve you," he said, and his throat burned. "You're a damn good friend."

The flicker of pain was so brief, it vanished before fully registering. She held his gaze a long moment before letting her hand fall to her side. "Call me."

"I will." But for now he had to go home, be there for his mother. Mac and Susan Jones may not have given him biological life, but they'd been the best parents Eric could imagine. They'd loved and supported him, given him room to make his own decisions and mistakes.

Now it was his turn to stand tall, be strong.

Eric put his hand to the doorknob and turned, stepped into the cool hallway of his apartment building. But he couldn't leave without seeing her one last time. Leigh. His friend.

"I'll be back," he promised, turning toward her.

She gave him a soft smile, but it didn't hide the tears shimmering in her calm brown eyes. "I'll be here."

Eric drank in the sight of her standing there, bathed in the early-morning sun, one of his sheets draped around her body, looking so beautiful the sight actually hurt. Forcing a smile, he leaned down and pressed a kiss to her forehead, then turned and walked away. He had a plane to catch and a father to bury.

Until then, he couldn't think about the heart he had to break.

One

"How long has it been? Eight years?"

Eric Jones popped the top on an ice-cold beer and handed the can to his surprise visitor. "Ten."

Jake Ingram let out a low whistle. "Time flies."

"In some ways," Eric acknowledged, closing the refrigerator. A lifetime had passed since he'd last lived in Chicago, but when he'd rounded the corner a few minutes before with the August sun beating down on him and a bag of groceries in hand, the sight of the tall, dark-haired man pacing outside his Lincoln Park brownstone had reduced a decade to a moment. He'd half expected to see Matt and Ethan lounging on the steps, Leigh with a backpack slung over her shoulder and a smile lighting her expressive brown eyes.

Leigh.

The five of them hadn't been together for ten years, not since the night his father had died. He'd had no idea those dark hours would become a stark delineation in his life—before and after. At twenty-five, he'd felt grown-up, mature, responsible. He'd been certain he knew where his future was going and how to take it there.

With vicious speed, he'd discovered otherwise. He'd been practically a kid that brutally cold night his mother had called from the hospital, but within weeks he'd learned what it meant to be a man.

"Have a seat," Eric said, leading Jake from the spartan kitchen of his fourth-floor apartment to the equally spartan living room, where ESPN blazed across the big-screen TV. He hadn't seen his old friend since Thanksgiving the year before.

Jake settled into a leather recliner. He looked damn good, had hardly changed since college. His hair was just as dark, with only a hint of gray settling in. There were a few more lines on his face, but that, Eric knew, was to be expected.

"Lincoln Park," he said with the devilish grin Eric remembered well. "You son of a bitch."

Eric laughed. "You're just jealous."

"Damn straight I am." Jake set his beer on an old sea chest that doubled as a coffee table. "The Cubs, the Bears, the Blackhawks, real pizza and authentic blues. You can't get any of that in Texas."

Eric shrugged out of his sport coat and sprawled out on his new sofa, also in distressed leather. "Hey, you've got the Cowboys," he pointed out dryly.

Jake practically growled. "Watch it."

Eric grinned. "No one's making you stay in your big house on the prairie," he reminded, but knew that wasn't true. His friend had deep ties to the Lone Star State: doting parents and a brother with whom he was tight, a fiancée who adored him.

The twinge of envy caught Eric by surprise. He'd always wanted a brother or a sister, but his parents had adopted only one child. He figured that was why he'd formed such strong friendships with Jake and Matt and Ethan.

And Leigh.

Over the years, he'd kept in touch with the guys, getting together occasionally. But he'd never seen Leigh after the night compassion had spiraled so hideously out of control. He'd only talked to her once, and that was to say goodbye.

She'd moved to England, never come home.

Glancing at his watch, Eric saw the hour approaching six. "How long are you in town?" he asked Jake.

"A few days."

"Great." He stood and headed for the phone. "If you're in the mood for torture, the Cubs are home. The firm has tickets behind the visitor's dugout. Let me see what I can—"

"Indy."

Normally, use of his college nickname, a play on his home state of Indiana and his last name, made Eric grin, but the gravity in Jake's voice stopped him cold. "Already got plans?" he asked, turning toward him.

His friend stabbed a hand through his thick dark hair. "A ball game sounds great," he said, and almost sounded angry. "You wouldn't believe how great. But actually I'm here on business."

Eric put down the phone. "Real business or World Bank business?"

Jake stood. "Crappy business."

Eric watched his friend closely, instinct suddenly warning that this was not a casual visit. The dead-serious look on his buddy's face sent a cold chill snaking through him.

"Jake?"

His jaw clenched and his eyes went dark, much as they had ten years before when some schmuck Leigh had turned down got revenge by spreading rumors that she was sleeping with Jake and Eric, as well as their buddies Matt Tynan and Ethan Williams. The Blues Brothers, they'd been called. They'd rallied to her defense, taught the punk a lesson Eric was sure he remembered to this day.

Christ, Leigh.

"Why don't you sit down?" Jake suggested.

"I don't like the sound of this," Eric said. The cold sinking through him turned insidious. "Is it Eth or Tynan? They in trouble?"

"They're fine," Jake almost growled, then moved toward the sofa, sat. "Come on, Indy. Sit."

Adrenaline crashed through Eric, but he did as Jake asked, if for no other reason than to get his friend to talk. "What's going on?"

Jake picked up the remote and zapped the television. "You've been following the World Bank heist investigation?"

Eric's tension eased a fraction. Whatever bomb his friend had to drop, it pertained to business. For over four months he'd been following Jake's progress as he and the federal government worked to solve the ultimate April Fool's joke—the theft of $350 billion from the influential World Bank. Achilles, they called the culprit who single-handedly had sent the stock market into decline and small banks into failure. Eric, an investment banker, had been dealing ever since with panicky clients, worried about the security of their college funds and retirement plans.

"Kind of hard not to, when your name and picture has been splashed across the newspaper on an almost daily basis." Even *The Wall Street Journal* was tracking Jake's progress. "Are you closer to finding Achilles?"

The planes of Jake's face tightened. "The son of a bitch has the FBI running in circles like a dog chasing its tail. He's planted endless dead-end trails and false leads."

That, Eric had heard. It blew his mind that hundreds of billions of dollars could simply vanish into thin air. "Do they think he was working alone?"

"No. They're pretty sure he's on someone's bankroll, probably a struggling eastern European country like Rebelia."

Images formed in Eric's mind of a once-beautiful country now torn apart by the ravages of civil war. "DeBruzkya? The guy believed responsible for the theft of all those jewels?"

Jake nodded. "The feds think he's planning something bigger, amassing a hefty bankroll for a grab for more power."

"But there's no evidence?" Eric guessed, reaching for his beer.

"Nothing concrete. Nothing they can nail him with."

For the first time, Eric realized the magnitude of responsibility sitting on Jake's shoulders. He wasn't just investigating the largest theft in history, he was tracking a potential madman who posed a risk to the entire free world. No wonder he'd put his wedding on hold.

"Christ, man, you're in deep, aren't you?"

Jake pinched the bridge of his nose, then met Eric's gaze. "The feds and I aren't seeing eye-to-eye anymore," he said levelly. "Daniel Venturi, the agent assigned to the case after the first agent, Lennox, went down, is an old-school hard-liner who sees this as his opportunity to make a lasting name for himself."

Eric rolled the beer can in his hands. "Not exactly an unassuming Fox Mulder type, I'm guessing."

A hard sound broke from Jake's throat "Hardly." He leaned forward and balanced his elbows on his knees. "Communication has broken down since he came onto the scene. At first I thought it was because Venturi doesn't appreciate an outsider being involved.''

"And now?"

Jake glanced toward the sliding glass door, then back at Eric. "Now I know it's because before Lennox died, a suspect surfaced. When Venturi took over, he was under instructions to hold quiet until the case was almost completely buttoned-up.''

The resentment in Jake's voice was impossible to miss. "Does that mean this mess is almost over?"

Jake frowned. "I'm afraid it's just starting.''

It wasn't like Jake to talk in circles. "How so?"

"Dammit," Jake said. "There's absolutely no easy way to tell you this. Their suspect, Eric. Their suspect is you.''

Eric went very still. "Come again?"

His friend stood, started to pace. "The feds, Indy. The feds have fingered you as the mastermind behind Achilles.''

The words hit him with the force of a sucker punch. He stared at this man he'd known over a decade and looked for a twinkle in his eyes or a twitch of his lips, any indication that Jake had developed a twisted sense of humor, but found only tight lines of frustration.

"That's ridiculous." Eric slammed his beer to the chest and surged to his feet. "I can't program my way out of a paper bag, much less hack into a secure system.''

Jake frowned. "I know that, and you know that, but right now that doesn't make a damn bit of difference.''

Incredulity blasted him. "Why me?" he bit out, fumbling savagely at the silk tie cutting off his oxygen flow. "Why would the feds even look at me?"

Up until six months ago, he'd been a banker in a small Indiana town. He couldn't imagine a lower-profile life.

"They're looking because someone wants them to," Jake said grimly. "Because you're my friend." His eyes glittered. "Ever since this investigation started, someone has been playing fast and loose with my life. Did you know my brother was kidnapped? That they thought Zach was me? Sought to silence him—*me*—before I could finger the real bastard behind Achilles?"

Eric just stared. It sounded as though his friend was discussing some complex action-thriller, not their lives.

"They want me off the case," Jake continued, clearly angry and agitated. "Whoever is behind the World Bank heist, they're well-connected and they're powerful, and they'll stop at nothing to make sure I don't expose their house of cards. Now, any claim I make of your innocence will be written off as friendship and loyalty."

"They're that scared you're going to find the real culprit?"

"They're that determined to make sure I don't. With the feds focused on you—"

"The real trail goes cold." Eric sucked in a rough breath. With stunning speed, pieces and implications clanked into place, hard and fast and with brutal clarity. "How bad is it? How strong a case do they have against me?"

"Strong enough that you need a lawyer. You need one now. That's why I'm here."

Eric had only been in trouble with the law once, when he'd been a cocksure eighteen-year-old mouthing off at a patrol officer. To teach him a lesson, the cop had hauled him to the station and processed him, forced him to call his parents, then thrown him into the lock-up with drunks and drug addicts and three punks brought in for starting a brawl at a local nightclub. Eric had never forgotten the disappointed look in his father's eyes when he'd picked him up, or the long, quiet ride back to their house. His father, president of the local bank, had convinced the cops not to press charges, but the impact of the night had stayed with Eric.

This was so much worse. He was almost glad his parents weren't around to see their son fingered as the prime suspect in the worst bank theft in history.

"A lawyer," he muttered. "Christ." He didn't even know any defense attorneys. "You really think that's necessary?"

"I wouldn't be here if I didn't."

Shock was slowly giving way to cold shards of anger, but Eric forced back both emotions. He needed a clear head. "Okay. I'll make a few phone calls," he said, opening a drawer for his address book, "see if I can come up with a recommendation."

"You don't need to make any phone calls," Jake said quietly. "You need Leigh."

Eric went very still. For just a heartbeat. Then he turned slowly, looked at his friend standing in front of the sliding glass door, the late-day sun streaming in behind him and casting him in silhouette. "What did you just say?"

Jake stepped into the shadow of an enormous banana plant. "I said Leigh, Eric. You need Leigh."

Her name came at him through a dark tunnel of time and space, blasted him like a gust of warm tropical air. He'd not heard it spoken aloud for close to ten years, not since shortly after she'd left for Oxford, when Jake and Ethan and Matt had ganged up on him and tried to convince him to go after her. Eric had been keeping everything bottled up inside, all his frustration and anger, the regret and guilt, the sense of helplessness he'd never before experienced. He'd exploded, slammed his fist through a wall and shocked his friends into silence. *Don't say her name to me*, he'd roared. *Just let it go.*

Like he'd let her go.

And they had.

Until now.

"She's here," Jake said quietly, walking toward Eric. "In Chicago. Practicing law, just like she always dreamed."

It was Eric's turn to shove a hand through his hair. "I'm not calling Leigh."

"Eric, think about—"

"I can just see it," he interrupted viciously, wanting to hit something, anything, but finding nothing within striking distance. "Hey, Leigh, babe, it's me, Indy. Yeah, yeah, I know. I haven't seen you since the night I took your virginity then left you cold and naked in my apartment, but hey, I'm in trouble now and was thinking we could get together, that you'd drop everything to help me out."

Jake's mouth fell open, forcing Eric to realize the extent of what he'd revealed. The guys had never known what had happened after they'd left his apartment. He'd been too appalled to tell them, and clearly Leigh had kept quiet, as well.

"That's right," he now said, anger feeling far better than helpless frustration. "I couldn't keep my hands off her, then went home and married someone else." He laughed bitterly. "I'm sure she'll be real damn happy to hear from me."

Jake squeezed his eyes shut, opened them a moment later. "You two need to talk."

"Didn't you hear a word I just said? I used her, Jake. I hurt her in ways she didn't come close to deserving."

"That was a long time ago," Jake said lamely. "We're older now. Life has gone on."

Life could never go on far enough to excuse what he'd done. "I'll find someone else."

"Leigh knows you. Whatever happened ten years ago can't change the friendship you shared before then. She knows what kind of a man you are, how deep your integrity runs. She knows you'd never commit a crime like this." He paused, pierced Eric with his stare. "I'm willing to bet she'll fight tooth and nail to make sure the rest of the world learns that about you, too."

Eric turned away, saw the past. Saw Leigh standing in front of the window of his small apartment, the white sheet clutched around her naked body, the vulnerability in her soft brown eyes, the snow flurries drifting lazily behind her.

That was the last time he'd seen her.

"She's your best chance," Jake encouraged from behind him.

Slowly, his gut twisting like barbed wire, Eric turned to face his friend. "Then I'm in big trouble."

"All clear."

Jake nodded at Robert, one of two plainclothes security personnel he'd hired after the attempt on his brother's life, then emerged from the secluded doorway of Eric's brownstone and walked toward the waiting black sedan. The FBI had wanted to provide protection, but Jake didn't want big brother watching his every step. He didn't want anyone watching. Especially now.

He'd even checked into his hotel under an assumed name.

The late-day sun blazed with vicious disregard from

a picture-perfect sky, combining with searing humidity to turn the city into a sauna. That was one thing he didn't miss about Chicago. Of course, Dallas in August wasn't much better, more like an oven than a sweat factory.

At a bar down the street, happy hour rollicked on. Music and laughter mingled and carried outside. Too easily he remembered a time when he and Eric, along with Matt and Ethan, had been the ones cutting up and carrying on.

It seemed like a lifetime ago.

In only a few short months, everything Jake thought he'd known about his life had proven to be a lie. He was living in a souped-up spy thriller and no matter how hard he fought to stay one step ahead, the road before him lengthened.

Eric Jones as a modern-day Jesse James, pulling off the largest theft in world history. What a joke.

Except it wasn't the least bit funny.

Jake knew damn good and well his friend, the personification of honor and loyalty, would never, could never, execute such a crime. But he also knew the forces working against them were powerful. Innocence didn't mean a damn thing.

That was why he walked past the sedan and continued down the street. He couldn't just sit in the back-seat and let someone drive him around, not when energy and adrenaline roiled around inside him. He needed to do something. Something other than issue dire warnings to a friend.

Something other than argue with his fiancée.

He should call her. He knew that. The last time they'd spoken she'd made no secret of her irritation with him, but with the oppressive heat bearing down on him, the last thing he wanted was to try to explain to Tara, one more time, that he needed her to be patient just a little while longer.

In truth, he no longer knew how to explain. From the moment he'd accepted the World Bank assignment, his life had careened down a crazy path. Through the course of the investigation, he'd learned more about himself, his past, than the theft.

Your life is a lie. You're not who you think you are.

When he let himself, he could still see the wild glint in the older woman's eyes as she'd passed him the note. At first, he'd written her off as a quack. He'd thought someone was trying to distract him from the investigation. But then the dreams had began, dark, disturbing, blurring the line between reality and fiction. He'd met with the woman—her name was Violet—several more times, listened in shock to her wild story, her claims that she was his birth mother and that he had brothers and sisters scattered across the country, that they were all in dire danger. She'd given him a key the last time he'd seen her.

Then she'd died.

Grief clutched him all over again. The authorities called the car crash that killed her an accident, but Jake had to wonder.

In the weeks since then he'd tracked down two of the siblings Violet had told him about, and the connection had been immediate. And intense. The shock of it all drilled deep.

He had a brother, a Navy SEAL named Marcus. And a sister—a twin. Gretchen was her name, and the moment he'd seen her, he'd known he'd finally found a piece of himself that had always been missing.

The key had led to a safe deposit box in Arizona, and

inside they'd found heavily coded notes. Gretchen was deciphering them now, and if Violet's incredible story about genetic engineering proved to be true, he had more siblings somewhere, living blissfully unaware of the danger stalking them. Violet claimed they carried hypnotic triggers deep in their subconscious, and that if the triggers fell into the wrong hands, they could become pawns, directed to use their superior skills to commit crimes.

Swearing softly, Jake unclipped his mobile phone from his belt and jabbed in a series of numbers. It took a moment before the connection was made, with static making hearing difficult.

"Jake?" came a soft female voice, one that made him smile despite the frustration coursing through him. "That you?"

"Hey, Gretchen," he said, and immediately his mood lightened.

"You still with Marcus?"

"No." He'd hated leaving his brother so soon after finding him, but the second he'd received the call about Eric, he'd known he had to leave. "I'm in Chicago. World Bank stuff."

"Oh."

He glanced at his watch, realizing how late it was in Brunhia, the remote island off the coast of Portugal where Gretchen and her husband had settled. Marcus would be traveling there soon. "I didn't wake you, did I?"

"Are you kidding?" she said with that soft, lilting laugh of hers. The one that sounded so damn familiar it made his chest tighten. "Who can sleep with all these disks to decode?"

Jake shoved a hand through his hair. He heard what

his sister didn't say. "Are the nightmares getting worse?"

She hesitated. The long-distance connection crackled. And still Jake waited.

"More intense," she finally said. "One minute I see children on a beach, laughing and building sand castles, and there's this incredible sense of belonging. Of happiness. But in the next…in the next there's an explosion and everything goes dark. There's screaming and water everywhere, fire, and…and I can't breathe."

Jake frowned. He was glad Gretchen had her husband, Kurt, with her. "I've had the same dream," he admitted, knowing it was no dream at all, but memory. For over twenty years, life before his thirteenth birthday had been a blank canvas, but now, with increasing speed and ferocity, images intruded. "Hang in there," he told his sister. "I've got to go for now."

"I'll let you know when I crack these disks."

"And I'll be in touch soon."

Just as soon as he found a way to prove Eric Jones and Achilles were not one and the same.

From a cloudless blue sky, the blistering sun presided over the snarl of rush-hour traffic. Summer in Chicago. There was nothing like it.

Sipping the iced latte she'd purchased from a coffee shop across from her office building, Leigh Montgomery waited to cross Michigan Avenue. During her years in the U.K., she'd forgotten the suffocating combination of searing heat and oppressive humidity, how it could choke you, make you long to strip off your clothes and jump into the nearest body of water.

Fleetingly, she glanced at a nearby fountain. The temptation made her smile.

She'd been only twenty years old that impossibly cold, starkly beautiful December morning when she'd boarded a plane for London, but in the ensuing years the girl had become a woman, the coed a seasoned attorney. Practicing law and dealing with the criminal element changed people.

So did a broken heart.

Briefcase slung over her shoulder, she crossed the street with a rush of pedestrians and cruised through the revolving doors of the high-rise where she'd been working for the past two years, ever since returning to the States and passing the bar. An elevator whisked her skyward, while she mentally inventoried her morning workload. She'd left the house later than she'd meant to, which had resulted in her arriving downtown forty-five minutes behind schedule. She had a brief to review, a few calls to make, and a new client scheduled after lunch. It would be tight, but she could swing it.

At the fifty-seventh floor, the steel doors slid open and Leigh stepped briskly into the stately reception area of Brightman and Associates. Thomas Brightman had a flair for appearances, and accordingly, the firm's decor conjured images of an old English manor house. The floor was a highly polished, gleaming mahogany, matching the receptionist's desk. Dark green covered the walls, save for the elaborate built-in shelves which housed an impressive collection of law books. The furniture was Chippendale, inviting no one to become too comfortable.

"Good morning, Jules," Leigh greeted, heading toward the corridor that housed her office. "Did I miss anything?"

"Actually, there's a gentleman waiting to see you."

Leigh glanced at her watch, saw the hour drawing near ten. "My first appointment isn't until one thirty."

"He says it's important."

Leigh frowned. It was always important. "He'll have to schedule a time and come back. I've got a mountain of work on my desk and nowhere near enough hours in the day."

Julia hesitated. "He's been waiting for over an hour."

"I'm sorry," Leigh said, and was. "But my morning is full. I don't have time for a walk-in—"

"Leigh."

Abruptly she stopped walking, stopped talking, stopped breathing. Even her heart stopped beating.

"It's me."

The quiet masculine voice came from behind her, not just a few steps, but miles and years. She stood very still for a long, punishing moment, ignoring the puzzled look on Julia's face and trying to convince herself her imagination was playing a cruel joke on her.

She knew that voice. She *remembered* that voice. She'd heard that voice at night in her dreams so many times over the years, heard it confidently debate economic theory, whisper words of passion and need, blandly tell her goodbye.

It couldn't be him. It couldn't. No way would he just stroll back into her life one day, even if he'd done so in her dreams countless times.

Correction. They weren't dreams.

They were nightmares.

Slowly, shoulders square and professional smile pasted in place, Leigh turned around.

And once again forgot to breathe.

Two

Ten years was a long time. People changed, life moved on. Old dreams faded and new ones took their place. Time never stood still.

But for Leigh, as she stood in the cool, quiet lobby of the staid law firm, staring at the tall man with the professionally cut sandy hair and piercing blue eyes, it was as though she'd never put an entire ocean between her and the past, never been with another man, never made decisions guaranteed to haunt her for the rest of her life.

Eric.

She'd imagined this moment countless times, had wondered what it would be like to see him, to feel the energy that rushed through her when he so much as entered the room. But nothing had prepared her for this. Nothing could possibly have prepared her to see him standing in the muted lighting of the reception area, looking at her through the eyes of the boy she'd once loved, but wearing the professional clothing of a man she did not know.

Every hot, shattered, humiliated emotion came cascading back, hard, fast and broken. But in the years that stood between them, the naive girl she'd been had grown up. Lessons hadn't come easily, but she'd learned, and standing there in the posh lobby of Brightman and Associates with her heart thudding painfully, Leigh refused to let one sliver of emotion seep through.

"Eric," she forced herself to say, breaking the uneasy silence. "This is quite a surprise."

He smiled slightly, just enough to reveal the dimple to the side of his mouth that had once made her heart thrum.

"It's been a long time," he said simply.

Nowhere near long enough.

The years had been kind to him, hardening the lines of his face and the intensity of his eyes, but preserving that thick hair that used to fall roguishly into his face during the economics class he'd taught on Tuesday and Thursday mornings. For a fleeting moment she was an undergrad again, sitting in the front row and trying to pay attention to his lecture, but instead fantasizing about what it would feel like to brush those unruly locks back from his forehead.

But that girl was gone now, all grown up.

And the grad student was a man with the power to shatter her world.

Shaking off the past, Leigh set her coffee on Jules's desk, then stuck out her hand. She was an attorney skilled at taking on prosecutors and judges. One man, the memory of one night, could not reduce her to a naive, love-struck college girl.

"I didn't know you were in town," she said in her best professional voice, the one that allowed a trace of her eight years in England to seep through.

Eric stared at her outstretched hand, the line of his mouth turning hard. Everything happened so fast then, she didn't have time to prepare herself. Didn't have time to move.

"Christ, Leigh," he muttered, but rather than accepting her gesture, he crushed her in his arms.

Shock streamed through her, ten years of heartbreak warring with an age-old longing. She was a seasoned attorney—a barracuda the English press had called her—a woman who didn't back down from cutthroat prosecutors or crusty judges. She'd learned to stand her ground, fight tooth and nail for her clients. But standing in Eric Jones's embrace, for a painful moment she felt small and vulnerable, fragile in a way she hadn't been in years. She could hear his heart beating, smell the masculine scent of sandalwood and clove that had never stopped haunting her.

The temptation to put her arms around him and hold him, just hold him, pierced like a physical pain.

"It's damn good to see you," he said against her hair, which she'd pulled back into a sleek silver barrette, in deference to the heat.

The words washed through her and around her, stripped away the years between them. But more than time separated them, Leigh reminded herself. Secrets and truths and lies all had their places as well. She was no longer the bright-eyed Pollyanna who'd once sat starstruck in this man's economics class. She'd learned to push forward despite adversity, separate truth from fantasy, protect herself from the ugliness she frequently encountered as a defense attorney. But more than anything, she'd learned to ignore the longing deep inside, the dangerous yearning to close her eyes and savor the feel of Eric's arms around her, to believe she and Eric Jones could ever get past one desperate, snowy night.

Suddenly unable to breathe, she struggled from his arms and stepped back. She could barely look at him, much less touch him without remembering that night a lifetime ago.

Or the morning after.

"Look," she said as levelly as she could, "I know it's been a long time, but now isn't a good time. My morning is full and—"

His expression hardened. "Don't, Leigh."

"Don't what?" Temper spiked. He'd been out of her life for ten years. He didn't have the right to stroll back in and expect her to drop everything for him. "If you'd like to schedule time next Monday or Tuesday, Julia will be glad to help."

He stepped closer, lowered his voice. "Don't shut me out."

"Shut you out?" she asked incredulously. "It's been ten years, Eric. Ten years without one word."

Of course, she hadn't tried to contact him, either. But then, she hadn't wanted to know. Hadn't wanted to hear about the house he and his wife Becky had bought, the family they were starting.

"I know," he said in a voice unusually thick. "And I'm sorry. But I can't change any of that. Not now."

Neither of them could. Every decision carried a consequence, and consequences had to be lived with. "Look, I've got to get on with my morning." She had to breathe, figure out what to say to this man, what to keep to herself. "Maybe we can get together sometime next week?"

A week wouldn't be long enough, but it would give her a few days to prepare. And decide.

His eyes darkened. "Next week is too late. I need you now."

The breath jammed in Leigh's throat, trapped by a sudden rush of alarm. It took effort, but she kept her expression unreadable while the impact of that simple statement wove through her with relentless disregard for the years between them. Her heart thrummed hard. Thoughts fractured.

She could only stare at Eric, try to understand the quiet ferocity blazing in his gaze.

The same ferocity she'd seen that desperate, snowy night ten years before.

The ferocity that still had the power to twist her up inside, make her ache in ways she'd thought long behind her.

Abruptly, she glanced at a clearly fascinated Julia. "We'll be in the conference room," she said, leveling the receptionist with her best don't-ask glare. No way was she escorting Eric Jones into her office, her personal space, where he'd learn truths she wasn't remotely ready to discuss.

With a calmness she didn't begin to feel, she motioned for Eric to follow her, then walked briskly down the plush carpet of the hallway, thankful the upholstered walls absorbed sound, even the hammering of her heart.

At the massive mahogany door, she didn't break stride, just depressed the handle and breezed inside. A long, gleaming table dominated the center of the room, with floor-to-ceiling bookcases occupying two walls. The third wall featured a credenza with a delicate demitasse coffee service below a window boasting a breathtaking view of Lake Michigan.

Needing a moment, she crossed the room and stared over the choppy blue water. In the distance a score of brightly colored sailboats moved lazily, almost imperceptibly, against an impossibly blue horizon. Come the weekend, that number would multiply.

"How long have you been back?" came Eric's voice from behind her.

Leigh tensed. "Two years," she said, turning to face him. "London was wonderful, but Chicago is home."

Eric's mouth curved in that easy, relaxed manner she remembered too well. "I know what you mean. I've been back six months. Bought a place in Lincoln Park."

Questions jumbled through her, but she refused to give them voice. Their answers didn't matter. How well Eric's wife, Becky, was adjusting to big-city life had no relevance to Leigh. "I'm up in Lake Forest."

Surprise registered in his gaze. "The burbs? I always pictured you as a high-rise girl."

"I'm not a girl anymore," she said automatically, but when his gaze heated and skimmed down her tailored taupe pantsuit, lingering on her chest before returning to her face, she realized her mistake. "The burbs suit me just fine."

"You look good," he said quietly. He stood several feet away, but the heat of his stare singed clear down to her bone.

She refused to step back, wasn't about to trap herself between his body and the window. "I'm happy."

"It shows," he said, then closed the distance between them. "How about this heat?" he asked, looking out over the lake.

And Leigh couldn't take it. She couldn't just stand there and make small talk with Eric Jones. Just looking at the man twisted her up inside. He stood so close now she could feel the warmth of his body merging with the warmth from the window, both of which made her long to take off her fitted jacket and unbutton her blouse a bit further.

"Look, Eric, I know what you're trying to do, but

let's not, okay? Let's not stand here and make small talk like we're old friends catching up on where life has taken us.''

He turned to face her. ''Aren't we old friends?''

No. Absolutely not. Old friends kept in touch over the years, exchanged Christmas cards, e-mails and an occasional phone call. Old friends conjured images of warmth and security, not this crazy jumble of emotions jostling around inside Leigh. Not this uncharacteristic vulnerability.

''You know what I mean,'' she said vaguely.

The disappointment in his gaze said that he did. ''Jake told me you've made quite a name for yourself as a defense attorney on both sides of the pond.''

Her smile was automatic. ''How is Jake?'' she asked, trying to recall the last time they'd spoken. It had been in April, shortly after he'd been tapped to investigate the World Bank heist. ''I haven't seen him in ages, except in the newspapers.''

''Have you been following the investigation?''

Frustration tightened through her. She really didn't know how to make idle chatter with Eric Jones. The last time she'd looked the man in the eye, she'd been standing cold and naked in one of his sheets. The last time she'd seen him, he'd been standing somberly between his mother and his fiancée, with his back to Leigh. He'd never even known she was there.

''Kind of hard not to,'' she said, glancing at her watch. ''Jake's really waded into a mess this time.''

''He's not the only one.''

There was an odd note to Eric's voice, a gravity that had not been there before. And deep inside, the tickle of discomfort intensified. The instincts of an attorney kicked hard. "Has something happened? Is that why you're here?"

Eric swore softly. "There's no easy way to say this," he muttered, shoving a hand through his hair.

And only then did Leigh note that a gold band did not circle his ring finger. There wasn't even a slight discoloration, hinting at skin that hadn't seen the sun in awhile. His hand was just as square and strong and tanned as always.

"Eric?"

"Jake came to see me yesterday," he bit out. "The feds have closed in on a suspect, are preparing for an arrest."

"It's about time," Leigh said. "Whoever this Achilles bastard is, he deserves to rot in jail for the rest of his life."

Something hot flashed in his eyes. "They think he's me."

Leigh stood very still, completely sure she'd somehow misunderstood him. "What?"

"The feds think I'm Achilles," he told her in a voice stripped of all the warmth of only minutes before. The words came out hard, angry. "Jake came to warn me, said the lead agent—Venturi, I think his name is—is convinced I'm their man."

Disbelief robbed Leigh of breath, merged with horror. The shock of seeing Eric fractured into something far worse. Since April the press had been full of stories about the far-reaching consequences of the ambitious crime, the fate awaiting the culprit, who, the FBI vowed, would be found and brought swiftly to justice. Careers in the upper echelons of the government lay on the line. An arrest needed to be made soon, or heads would roll.

But not Eric. Dear God, not Eric.

"That's ridiculous," she said through the tightness in her throat.

"You know that," he bit out, shoving his hands into the pockets of his gray trousers. "I know that and Jake knows that, but the FBI thinks otherwise." He paused, searched her gaze. "That's why I'm here."

I need you...

No, he didn't. Not her.

She turned from him, from the intimacy of the deep, eye-to-eye contact, and glanced out the window, not at the lake that made her think of dreams and fantasies, but at the congested snarl of cars and taxis and buses fifty-seven stories below.

Eric Jones needed an attorney, and while she couldn't fulfill that role for him, she was safer operating in that mode, than in the mode of a woman facing the man she'd once loved with all her heart, the man who'd apologized for the night they'd made love, then encouraged her to move to Oxford as he calmly announced he was going through with his plans to marry his high-school, middle-school, grade-school sweetheart.

The man who no longer wore a wedding ring, but whom the feds had set in their sights.

"Try not to worry," she said. "I've worked on cases involving the FBI before, and if there's one thing I've learned, it's that they don't play footsie." They played to win. "If an arrest is made, it's only because they have ironclad evidence." Even the best defense barely stood a chance against the FBI, not when the resources of the entire government had been brought to bear to make sure the guilty party was arrested. Federal prosecutors rarely lost cases, hated to be made fools of.

"They may be sniffing around," she said, looking

back at him with a reassuring smile, "but I'm sure they'll realize they've got the wrong man and move on."

The lines of tension on Eric's face lessened. "I want to believe that, but it's not a chance I can take. I have to be prepared. I need to know that if the worst comes to pass, you'll be there for me. I need to know you'll be my attorney."

The breath whooshed right out of Leigh. "I'm afraid that's impossible," she said. She could barely look at him without remembering the feel of his mouth on hers, their bodies moving together, the devastation of his casual dismissal. She could not be the one he turned to in his time of need, not with the history and heartbreak and secrets standing between them. She couldn't imagine a more surefire prescription for disaster.

Surprise and disappointment flashed hard in the deep blue of his eyes. "Is this because of what happened the night my dad died? Is that why you're not willing to help?"

The room started to spin. She was not letting him do this to her, not letting him drag her back ten years in time. It took more than memories to break her.

"I'm too personally involved," she explained in her best professional voice, but almost choked on the understatement. "The best I can do is find someone else to help."

His gaze held hers. "No," he said quietly. "I need you."

The intensity in his eyes sent her reeling. "Eric—"

"You know me," he rolled on. "You *are* personally involved. How can that be a bad thing?"

Because she couldn't think straight around him. She could barely breathe.

"It's not as simple as that," she explained. "You

need to trust me on this one. You'll be better off with someone else.''

Fleetingly, she glanced at his bare ring finger, then back to his face. Only moments before a hot blue fire had burned in his eyes, but they were flat now, completely detached.

''Apparently so,'' he said in a harsh voice. ''I can see I've wasted your time.''

''Eric, please understand—''

''I understand,'' he bit out. ''I understand perfectly.''

That said, he turned and strode across the conference room, pulled open the massive door, then vanished into the hallway.

Leigh watched him go, felt her chest tighten all over again. Once upon a time Eric Jones had filled every corner of her young heart. There hadn't been a thing in the world she wouldn't have done for him. She'd known his devotion lay elsewhere and that he would never return her feelings, but that hadn't lessened her desire to have him in her life. Their time together had seemed magical, even when they'd done something mundane like debate economic theory. And his smiles. Dear God, when he'd give her one of those warm, endearing smiles, everything inside had turned soft and warm.

One night had changed everything.

They could never go back, Leigh knew. Maybe she and Eric would share some kind of acquaintance in the future, but it would never be the easy, uncomplicated camaraderie they'd once enjoyed. That time was over. Those people were gone. Life had taken them down radically different paths, and even if they were both in Chicago, proximity could not take away what stood between them.

Nothing could.

He wouldn't be arrested, she told herself as she left the conference room. He didn't need her. The FBI was just rattling cages. Soon they would move to their next target, and life would resume its normal cadence, as though the past thirty minutes had never happened.

But as she stepped into her cool, spacious office and saw the 8x10 mahogany frame seated on her credenza, the mischievous blue eyes, gap-toothed grin and irrepressible dimple staring back at her, she recognized the thought—the fleeting fantasy—for the impossible lie it was.

Eric Jones was back.

Nothing would ever, could ever, be the same.

Eric stepped from the revolving door and into the blistering mid-morning sun. The heat radiating from the concrete made the sidewalk feel like a bed of hot coals, but the discomfort paled in comparison to the punishment of seeing Leigh again.

Damn, he'd screwed that up.

Almost viciously, he tore off his sports coat and slung it over his shoulder, kept his pace brisk. Already, he could feel the cotton of his button-down shirt turning damp and clinging to his back and shoulders. The humidity choked like the noose he felt closing around his throat.

Mistake number one—going to Leigh in the first place. He never should have let Jake talk him into it. He and Leigh shared a past that could not be dissolved with a casual smile.

Mistake number two—a hug. Eric didn't know what kind of fool notion had possessed him to pull Leigh into his arms and hold her as though not a day had passed since the evening they'd started out laughing over pizza and beer. He'd known she wouldn't break into a wide smile and throw her arms around him the way she would greet Jake or Ethan or Matt, but then he'd seen her and common sense had fractured into something hard and unrecognizable.

He'd known she would mature into a spectacular woman, but nothing had prepared him for the sight of her walking confidently off the elevator with an expensive briefcase slung over her shoulder and a cup of gourmet coffee in her hand. Her hair was still long and dark and silky, pulled off her face in that damningly sexy barrette, baring her model-worthy cheekbones. And her eyes. Have mercy, her eyes. They were even more smoky than he remembered, with a touch of sophistication and womanly confidence that had not been there ten years before.

A stranger, he'd told himself. This woman was a stranger. But when she'd turned and looked him in the eye, when she'd coolly stuck out her hand in greeting, something inside him had snapped, and he'd been unable to stand there and pretend they'd never meant anything to each other.

That was what he should have done, though. He should have just taken her hand. That was the appropriate greeting, and even that was more than he deserved. He should never have pulled her into his arms.

Mistake number three—believing their past relationship had any relevance today. True, once they'd shared a special friendship, one steeped in trust and respect, but he'd crushed that bond by taking her to bed, then walking away. Life had jettisoned them in different directions since then, a fact driven home by the remote look in her eyes when she'd dismissed his request for help.

Leigh Montgomery had been there for him once before, and in return he'd used her badly. The woman she'd become was not interested in a repeat performance.

He couldn't say that he blamed her.

Three strikes, and he was out.

Eric stopped walking at a crowded intersection, just barely noticing that the light had turned red. Tourists and professionals pooled around him, waiting for the signal to cross. Down Michigan Avenue, a horn blared impatiently. In front of him, a bus whizzed by.

Going to see Leigh had been wrong. He hadn't known what kind of reception to expect, but as she'd gazed at him through those cool, detached, lawyerly eyes, he'd realized with painful clarity that she was no longer the carefree undergrad with the intelligent questions, warm smiles and quiet friendship. She was a woman now, all grown up. He had no idea what twists and turns her life had taken, but instinct warned there'd been many.

The light turned green and the crowd surged across the street, but Eric stood completely still. The last time he'd been with Leigh Montgomery, they'd been in bed, her naked and soft and willing, holding him, speaking softly, warming him in ways he hadn't known possible.

One moment, he thought savagely, turning to hail a taxi. His office was over a mile away. If he kept walking, he'd be soaking wet in time for his lunch appointment.

A shiny yellow cab pulled over and Eric slid inside, bit out the address of his office, then sat back and absorbed the feel of hot air blowing in from an open window. One moment, he thought again. It never ceased to blow his mind the power of one moment, one decision.

Living in the same city wouldn't change anything. They were strangers now. Friends might not let friends drive drunk, but strangers didn't much give a damn if the FBI came knocking.

Ten minutes later he stepped off the elevator into the quiet reception area of his brokerage firm. Unlike the elegance of Brightman and Associates, Yearling Investments boasted comfortable couches and a coffee table littered with investing magazines and the latest edition of *The Wall Street Journal.*

"Good morning, Barb," he greeted the receptionist who enjoyed playing mother hen to the brokers, despite the fact she was at least ten years their junior. "Any calls?"

"A few." She looked up from her computer monitor. "I put them into your voice mail."

"Great." Eric headed toward his office, drinking in the feel of the cool air conditioning. Maybe by the time lunch arrived, he'd be able to tolerate the thought of slipping on his sports coat.

"Eric?" Barb asked, and he paused. "There's a gentleman waiting to see you."

In no mood to deal with a panicky investor, Eric bit back his frustration and turned toward the waiting area, where a dark-haired man stood waiting.

"Daniel Venturi," the man said, stepping forward and flipping open a leather wallet. The shiny badge needed no explanation. "FBI."

"The World Bank heist? And you said no?"

Leigh didn't need to be skilled in interpreting body language to recognize the managing partner's displeasure. Frowning, she put down her second cup of coffee and closed the brief she'd been trying to review. "I have my reasons."

"Then perhaps you'd like to explain them to me."

She could barely think straight, much less explain to Thomas Brightman why she'd turned down a stab at what the press was billing the case of the century. The shock of seeing Eric lingered, refused to fade. Her whole body still burned from it, even as deep inside, she trembled.

So many times she'd wanted to ask Jake or Ethan or Matt about him, find out how he was doing, how his mother was, if he'd been able to salvage the family bank, but she'd never been able to force the words past the tightness in her throat. The guys were too perceptive. If she asked too much, if they heard the ache in her voice, she'd feared they would figure out the secret she'd kept, even from them, all these years.

But now... Seeing him again had been like looking into a distorted carnival mirror and seeing all that could have been, but wasn't. Seeing him hurt. Seeing him reminded her of choices drenched in heartache and decisions that could not be turned back from.

"Leigh?" Thomas asked. "You okay?"

She blinked, forced a smile. "You'll have to trust me on this one," she said. "I'm not the right attorney for Eric Jones."

No way could she represent him, when she could barely stand to look at him. Now that he'd strolled back into her life, she faced a monumental decision, one that could turn the achingly familiar warmth in his dark-blue eyes into shards of ice.

"I never took you for a coward, Leigh," Thomas said, rubbing his hand along his jaw as he always did when deep in thought. "Don't you realize what a case like this could do for our firm?"

She did. The publicity would be like a shot of adrenaline. But working with Eric Jones day in and day out would shred her in ways she never wanted to experience again. It was better that they not be knee-deep in a legal drama when the truth came spilling out and she and Eric were forced to confront, ten years too late, the consequences of one out-of-control night.

"He won't be arrested," she said, glancing furtively at the gap-toothed nine-year-old grinning at her from the familiar mahogany frame. *Please God, don't let him be arrested.*

"But if he is," Thomas persisted. "If the man is arrested, Brightman and Associates isn't going to run from this case."

Run. The word made her back stiffen. She hated to think that was what she'd done all those years ago, when she'd been a frightened, overwhelmed, heartbroken twenty-year-old with a child growing in her belly and a scholarship waiting at Oxford.

"Cal Myers or Linda Miller could take it," she suggested.

Thomas's brows knit together, just as they did when he was dominating a courtroom with one of his infamous closing arguments. He was one of the most brilliant, persuasive attorneys she'd ever met. "You're the one Jones knows," he said slowly. "You're the one he trusts, the one he wants. Is something else going on here? Some reason you don't feel capable of taking this case?"

This time she refused to glance at the picture of Connor. Her son. *Eric's son.* "I'm too personally involved."

"There's no law against that," Thomas pointed out. "In fact, personal involvement often strengthens the passion of commitment. If anyone would be dedicated to clearing this man's name, it would be you."

"He won't be arrested," she said again, but the

words, no matter how much vehemence she injected into them, did nothing to ease the chill snaking through her.

Thomas glanced at his Rolex, then sighed and pulled on his perfectly tailored gray pinstripe suit jacket. "If you believe he's innocent," he said, heading for the door, "I don't see how you can turn him down when the feds are closing in. A good attorney never backs down from a challenge." Before leaving, he paused for the killing blow. "I'm sure you'll make the right decision."

Leigh turned as the door closed and crossed to the wall of windows overlooking the north side of town. Several blocks away lay Lincoln Park, the network of quaint streets and turn-of-the-century brownstones Eric had always talked about. He lived there now, just a ten-minute drive away.

I need you.

God, she'd needed him, too, so badly the ache had eaten at her like a disease. She'd needed him to hold her when she'd almost miscarried in her third month, promise her everything would be okay. She'd needed him by her side in the delivery room, when his son had arrived breech. She'd needed him that horrible foggy morning Connor had awoken with a fever of 104 degrees.

She'd needed him so many times, in so many excruciating ways. She'd needed his smile and his laughter, his steady reassurance, his love.

But the latter had never been hers to have.

Damn it, Leigh, I'm sorry, he'd told her that frigid morning four weeks after his father's death. Four weeks after they'd created a child. *You've been such a good friend to me, and look how I paid you back. I was out of my mind, not thinking clearly and…Christ, I don't know. It just happened. I'd take it back if I could, you*

*have to know that. I'd make it all go away. But I can't
do that. Please, Leigh. Don't let that night change anything. You've got such a bright future ahead of you.
Oxford is waiting. You need to accept that scholarship…*

She had.

And he'd stayed in Cloverdale, with his mother and
Becky.

Leigh closed her eyes against the wash of pain, the
sharp blade of truth. Their lives had intersected once
again, separated now by city blocks rather than an ocean.
But something as simple as a short car drive could never
bridge the years, the distance, the secrets festering between them.

Nothing could.

Late-afternoon sun glinted through the windows of
Eric's apartment. They'd told him to sit, but he couldn't
just kick back while an army of FBI agents methodically
and relentlessly tore apart first his office and now his
home.

They'd pretty much covered both aspects of his life.

The noose he'd felt settle around his neck the day
before pulled tighter. Special Agent Venturi was the con-
summate professional, treating Eric with a kindness and
respect he knew better than to trust. These men were not
his friends. They were not on his side. Any casual question they asked masked a hidden agenda to lure Eric into
some kind of hideous trap.

He knew better than to take the bait.

So he held quiet. And watched. That was about all he
could do. Venturi didn't want him making phone calls,
and in truth, Eric didn't know whom to call. He wasn't
used to asking for help. He was usually the one doling
it out. He could call Jake, he knew. Jake was staying at

the Four Seasons and Eric had his cell number, but Eric figured he'd wait until after the wrecking crew left, when he knew more.

He sure as hell wouldn't be calling Leigh. She'd made it clear she wanted nothing to do with him, wouldn't lift a finger to help.

He couldn't say he blamed her.

"Venturi!" an agent called from the hall leading to Eric's bedroom. "We've got something!"

Adrenaline kicked through Eric. No way could they have something. No way. He pivoted and strode toward the triumphant-looking agent, but Venturi blocked his path. "Stay here."

"This is my home, damn it."

"And we have a search warrant. It's in your best interest to cooperate fully."

"What the hell do you think I've been doing?" Eric demanded.

Venturi met his gaze. "I know it's been a long afternoon, but you'll only be making matters worse for yourself if you rock the boat now."

"Rock the boat?" Eric bit out. He wanted to hit something, to slam his fist against the exposed brick wall of his brownstone, but he didn't stand close enough. "This is my life you're picking apart."

Venturi glanced toward one of two uniformed patrol officers who'd accompanied them to Lincoln Park. "Make sure Jones stays here," he said, then turned and disappeared down the hall.

Eric swore viciously. The air conditioning blasted full force, but he felt as if he were standing in an oven and someone had just cranked the temperature higher. He could feel perspiration break out on his body as his pulse kicked up.

He was an innocent man, but with brutal clarity he realized that might not mean a damn thing.

Moments later Venturi returned. Behind him, three stone-faced agents followed, the first carrying his laptop, the second carrying plastic bags containing books Eric had never seen before. And the third, the oldest and by far most sympathetic-looking of the three, carried a box containing Eric's banking and investment records.

Rage and panic twisted through him. "Where the hell did those come from?" he demanded, striding forward and gesturing toward the books he now saw were computer programming manuals. "You can't just take my computer!"

Special Agent Venturi glanced at the uniformed cop, then back at Eric. His eyes were black and cold, accusing. And Eric knew. God help him, he knew.

"Eric Jones," Venturi said in a hard, satisfied voice, "you're under arrest for the theft of three hundred fifty billion dollars from the World Bank."

The room started to spin. "This is bullshit!" Eric roared, but Venturi kept right on.

"You have the right to remain silent," he added, as the patrol cop grabbed Eric's arms and pulled them behind his back. Animal instinct urged him to rip away, to put up some kind of fight, but he knew enough about criminal procedure to know he didn't need a resisting-arrest charge thrown at him, as well.

"Anything you say can and will be used against you in a court of law. You have the right to an attorney…"

Three

"Jake, you promised."

Alone in his hotel room, Jake frowned. "I know, Tara, and I'm sorry, but this can't be helped."

"That's what you've been saying for months now," she persisted. "All I'm asking for is a date. Is that so very much?"

No. It wasn't. Jake knew that. But he also knew he wasn't in a position to plan a wedding, not when his life was blowing up around him. He didn't even know who he was anymore. He was the product of some bizarre genetic experimentation. He had brothers and sisters who'd been kept from him. They were being hunted. One by one, meticulously and relentlessly. His birth mother had been murdered within weeks of Jake learning who she was. His adoptive brother had been kidnapped. And now Eric.

"Jake, are you listening to me?" Tara demanded in a soft Texas drawl that hid a core of steel.

"I'm here," he said. He just didn't know how to tell his orderly, practical-minded fiancée the truth of who and what he was. Didn't know if he should. Didn't know if she could handle it, didn't know if she'd be safe.

So for now, he held quiet. "Things are complicated," he tried to explain. "The investigation has taken a turn and—" He paused when his mobile phone started to ring. Frowning, he picked it up and glanced at the text window, feeling his whole body tighten. "I'm sorry," he said abruptly, "but something's come up. I've got to go."

"Jake, wait!"

"I'll call you later," he promised, then disconnected the line and clicked on his mobile. A bad, bad feeling snaked through him. "Ingram."

Five minutes later, he dropped the phone and slammed his palm against the dainty Louis XIV desk.

So help him God they weren't going to get away with this.

The room was small and hot and smelled like antiseptic and fresh cigarette smoke. The pale-green walls seemed to shrink with each minute that ticked by. The bitter coffee on the small table had long since gone cold. Several minutes before, Venturi and two other agents had finally realized Eric had meant what he said. He wasn't going to talk until he had counsel.

Now he stood alone.

He also stood accused of the largest bank theft in history, an act the press had dubbed the crime of the century.

The media had been waiting for them the second the little caravan arrived downtown, a swarm of local and network affiliate reporters and photographers jockeying for position and a story. They'd shouted questions as Venturi hustled him inside.

"Why'd you do it?" a kid who didn't look old enough to be out of journalism school asked.

"How did you pull it off?" another wanted to know.

"Where's the money?"

Swearing at the memory, Eric slammed his palm against the wall, not giving a damn who might be watching through the two-way mirror across the room. He was an innocent man. He lived a simple life. He put coins in parking meters and paid his taxes on time.

None of that seemed to matter.

The feds thought they had their man. They'd been so cocksure upon leaving his apartment, full of back slaps and hearty congratulations. They'd brought him downtown, where he'd gone through booking like the drug dealers and murderers who routinely made their way through the Cook County system. He'd been photographed and fingerprinted, relieved of his personal possessions and his dignity. He'd been searched, given an orange jumpsuit, then led to this small dank room, where Venturi and two other agents had been waiting.

Instinct told Eric they expected him to be here for a while.

But he was alone now, left by himself to think, probably. To ponder his story. But he had no story, only the truth. He didn't have a damn thing to do with stealing billions from the World Bank. He didn't have a clue how to hack into a computer system. He'd never heard of a man named Achilles, until the name began appearing in newspaper articles.

...they're well-connected and they're powerful, and they'll stop at nothing to make sure I don't expose their house of cards.

Eric closed his eyes and breathed deeply, tried to relieve the hideous tightness of his chest. He had no idea what time it was. Well past midnight, he figured, but they'd taken his watch, so he had no way to know for sure.

From behind him, he heard the door open, then close. He waited for the sound of heavy footsteps approaching the table, but heard nothing, only a silence that seemed to buzz and pulse.

Anger pushed aside common sense. "I meant what I said, damn it," he insisted, spinning around. "I'm not saying a word until—"

He stopped midstride, midsentence. And stared.

She stood just inside the doorway, long dark hair loose around her face, her smoky gray pantsuit accentuating the paleness of her complexion. She wore little makeup, as though she'd just rolled from bed. Her eyes were huge, dark, almost bruised. And her gaze held a gravity that ripped clear down to his soul.

"Leigh," he somehow managed, hating how hoarse his voice had become. "What are you doing here?"

Her eyes met his. "Jake called me."

Jake. He should have known. "I told him not to do that." An impotent fury unlike anything he'd ever known hammered through him. "I told him to find someone else."

Leigh's mouth twisted. "There is no one else," she said softly, then moved to deposit her briefcase on the small metal table. "How are you holding up?" she asked, visibly inspecting him. "Are you okay?"

The sight of her in this small, miserable room twisted him up inside. Bright, vibrant Leigh didn't belong in a dark and dirty place like this.

"I don't want you here," Eric growled, moving toward her. He didn't understand the sudden spurt of anger, just knew he didn't want her dragged out of bed in the middle of the night, didn't want her in this awful place filled with lowlifes who would see her, contaminate her by their very presence. And God, he didn't want her seeing him like this, with his back to the wall and a degrading orange jumpsuit covering his body. "Please just go."

She didn't move a muscle. "I'm not going anywhere, Eric."

He stopped and curled his hands around the back of a chair. He wanted to keep right on going, to close the distances between them and...

He didn't know what. Part of him wanted to escort her to the door, tell her to leave and not look back, to go on with her life. Just what he'd told her ten years before. But the rest of him, the part in the majority, wanted to crush her in his arms and breathe in the clean, fresh scent of her hair, discover if she still used a shampoo that smelled of green apples, to hold on tight and this time never let go.

"This is bullshit," he roared. He was a man who prided himself on staying cool under pressure. He took charge when others faltered, made sense out of chaos. That was what he'd done his entire life. That's why he'd stayed in Cloverdale after his dad had died. That was why he'd told Leigh goodbye. Because his mother and Becky had needed him, and there'd been no one else.

But now he was the one with a need, and for the first time in his life, he flat-out didn't know what to do. He'd never allowed himself to need before, didn't know how to handle the twisted wreckage inside him, didn't know how to lean on someone else.

Especially Leigh.

"Eric," she said softly. "It's going to be okay. I promise you that."

There was a strength to her voice, a note of confidence that should have soothed. Instead, he felt the animal inside pull against chains of restraint. When confronted with Venturi's hostile questions and the sneers of the press, he'd held his composure, but now, in the face of Leigh's sudden appearance, of her belief, he wanted to pick up the heavy wooden chairs and throw them against the wall, upend the small table, see the stale coffee pool on the floor.

It didn't make a damn bit of sense.

"Those sons of bitches think I stole three hundred fifty billion dollars," he told her, and felt his eyes burn with fury.

"I've never even stolen a pack of gum," he bit out, shoving the hated, out-of-control feeling down deep. "The closest I've come is keeping a Mike Schmidt rookie card I found under a library table when I was in the third grade."

A small smile curved Leigh's mouth and warmed her chocolate eyes, transforming her, for the briefest of moments, into the girl he remembered. The one he'd looked forward to seeing every Tuesday and Thursday morning as he walked toward the economics class he taught. The one he'd allowed closer than a grad student should ever allow an undergrad.

Then she looked away. "You haven't told them anything, have you?" she asked, opening her briefcase and taking out a black-and-white composition notebook.

He watched her retrieve a heavy Mont Blanc pen and write his name at the top of a page, then jot a few notes. Her script was sleek and elegant, much as it had been before. Her hand was every bit as fine-boned. Pianist's hands, he remembered telling her a long time ago, to which she'd smiled. *Guilty, as charged,* she'd said, laughing.

The memory, the words, burned in ways he'd never imagined.

"You think they'd use the baseball card against me?"

he asked dryly, needing to defuse the tension that had them both acting like stick figures.

"Not that," she said, looking up from her notes.

He smiled warmly, wanting her to see that he was back in control. That he wasn't going to do something stupid like trash the interrogation room.

For a moment she just looked at him, looked hard. Then she smiled, too. It was slow and warm and it damn near socked him in the solar plexus. Suddenly he was twenty-five again and she was twenty, and he wanted to reach out and touch her, streak a finger down her cheek and see if her flesh would be as soft as it looked. As soft as he remembered.

Abruptly she stepped back as though she'd read his mind and didn't much like his thoughts. "I meant about the case," she clarified, glancing at her notebook. Long dark hair created a tangled curtain falling toward the table and concealing her face. "You haven't talked with the police or the feds about the theft, have you?"

Eric just stared. He stood accused of stealing billions, but for a moment, all he could think about was the fact that Leigh Montgomery had come for him in the middle of the night, and she hadn't even taken the time to comb her hair. He knew she was right. They needed to focus on the case. And he would. But for now he couldn't stop wondering who the hell this woman was. She looked like the girl he remembered and acted like the poised attorney he knew she'd become. But she wasn't turning her back on him, as he deserved.

"Eric?" she asked, glancing up.

Very slowly, very deliberately, he met her eyes with his own and answered her question. "Not without you."

"Good," she said, not looking away as she had before. Resilience glowed in her eyes and stole his breath.

"Let's get you out of here," she said briskly, then surprised him yet again. Her lips twitched. "Orange is not your color."

Three million dollars. The astronomical figure made Leigh's blood boil. "Bail is not supposed to be used as punishment," she growled as they left the police station through a back entrance. An army of hungry reporters swarmed the front lobby. "I've seen judges grandstand before, but this goes beyond ridiculous."

"It's okay," Eric said quietly, pushing open a steel door and holding it for her.

She stepped into the searing stickiness of late morning. The sun beat down from a hazy blue sky while Lake Michigan contributed its usual humidity, making the alley feel like a steam oven.

Leigh automatically shrugged out of the fitted jacket of her pantsuit. "No, it's not okay," she said. "I'm going to file a complaint as soon as I get into the office. There's no way you deserve a bail that high. You have no criminal record. You're an upstanding citizen. You're not a flight risk."

Eric reached down and relieved her of her briefcase, but said nothing. Just walked.

Deep inside Leigh, something twisted. Seeing him like this threw her back in time ten years, to the only other time she'd seen him fighting to stay in control. His normally piercing blue eyes were dark and flat, the planes of his face tight, his mouth a grim line. Whiskers emphasized the angry set of his jaw. His clothes were the same ones he'd worn to her office yesterday morning.

"I'm parked around the block," she told him, needing to say something, anything, to keep the silence from growing too deep. He'd barely said two words since they'd entered the courtroom for the arraignment and the preliminary charges had been read. The federal prosecutor had argued vehemently against bail, but Leigh had argued just as vehemently that Eric was innocent until proven guilty. She'd felt Eric stiffen at the pronouncement of three million dollars, but he'd said nothing. Only when Jake tried to supply the funds did Eric protest, and even then he'd only said no. But the way he'd bitten the word out, the hard finality to his voice and the cool glitter to his eyes, Jake and Leigh had realized he wasn't changing his mind.

Eric Jones had always been the strong one, the responsible one, the one to bail others out of a jam. He didn't know how to operate with the tables turned. He'd scraped together the required ten percent using proceeds from the sale of his father's bank in Indiana. He'd hotly protested Jake's offer to guarantee the remaining ninety percent with the deed to his ranch in Texas, but in the end, there'd been little choice.

If Eric ran, Jake would lose a small fortune.

Exhaling deeply, Leigh glanced across the street toward a Starbucks, but as much as she craved a latte, as much as she needed caffeine, she wanted Eric out of the public glare even more. He was like the walking wounded, whether he admitted it or not.

"Everything's going to be okay," she said for the hundredth time. God, what she wouldn't have given for a breeze off the lake. They'd only been outside five minutes and already her clothes stuck to her body. Not for the first time she wished she'd pulled her heavy hair back into a barrette, but in her haste to get downtown, she'd given little thought to detail.

She'd been in bed when Jake had called, but far from asleep. There'd been no way to drift off after having seen Eric for the first time in ten years. Her son's father. Who hadn't been wearing a wedding ring.

All those years between them, all the pain and heartbreak, the resolutions and determination to forget, had crumbled the second she'd heard his voice. His voice, damn it. That was all it had taken to erase a decade of hurt.

No way could she turn her back on an innocent man, especially the man she'd once loved with all her heart. The father of her son. She knew that, even if the voice of self-preservation insisted she do just that. Any doubt had fled the second she'd seen him in that degrading orange jumpsuit. He hadn't deserved that. It hadn't been necessary. But it told her the feds had expected him to remain in custody. It also told her somebody was showboating for the media and their superiors and God only knew who else.

"The burden of proof is on the government," she told Eric as they crossed the street toward her nondescript Toyota Camry, the dark-gray sedan she'd cleansed of bubble-gum wrappers and baseball cards shortly after midnight. "The government has to convince the jury of guilt beyond a shadow of doubt. That's a high standard in any case, but even higher when you're innocent."

They reached her car and she went to unlock the passenger door, but Eric's hand closed down on hers.

Startled, she turned and looked up at him, too late realizing she was trapped between his big body and the car. There was an intensity to his gaze, a glimmering light in his dark-blue eyes that had not been there before. And her heart hitched.

The longing ripped in from nowhere, tightening her throat and stealing her breath. Yesterday this man had stepped out of her memories and walked back into her life after a ten-year absence. He'd pulled her into his arms as if not a day had passed, not a tear had been shed, and held her the way she might expect a dear friend to. She'd heard his heart beat, smelled the sandalwood she'd never forgotten. But she had not hugged him back.

Now she wanted nothing more than to put her arms around him, hold him tight, promise him everything would be okay. *Make* everything okay. She wanted him to know she would be there for him, even if seeing him, hearing his voice, touching him, shattered her in ways from which she'd never recover.

But Eric didn't move. He just stood there with his hand on hers and the late-morning sun blazing down on them both, looking at her with an unnerving combination of warmth and puzzlement in his eyes.

"Why are you looking at me like that?" she managed.

He lifted a hand to her face and eased the hair from her cheek. "I'm trying to figure out who you are."

The breath stalled in her throat. "Pardon?"

"When I first saw you yesterday," he said in a raspy voice that made her insides go soft, "I saw Leigh, the smiling, intelligent girl who always sat in the front row of my economics class. And it felt so damn right." He paused as a group of tourists bounded by. "But then that girl was gone and I saw a stranger, this beautiful, elegant, reserved attorney whom I didn't know, had never seen before."

Who'd coldly turned her back on him.

He didn't say the words, but Leigh heard them loud and clear. "Eric—"

He slid a finger to her mouth, blocking her words. "Now I look at you," he said, his voice pitched low, "and I don't see the girl from before, but I don't see the stranger either." He paused, his gaze focused on her. "I have no idea who you are."

Deep inside, something broke and gave way. How many nights had she dreamed of Eric looking at her like this, with his eyes all hot and concentrated? How many nights had she lain in bed and tried to remember the resonance to his voice, the way it could seep through her like an intoxicating mist?

The temptation to step closer flowed through her like the echo of a forgotten dream, to lift her hand to his face as well, to feel those golden whiskers beneath her fingertips.

"I'm Leigh," she said softly, uncomfortable with the thickness to her voice. She had to keep her walls tacked high and strong around this man. They shared more than just a past. They shared a child. "I'm the woman who's not going to let you take the fall for a crime you didn't commit."

Eric stepped closer. The sun glared hotter. "Is that my attorney talking, or my friend?"

Oh, God. The coming days and weeks promised to be hard enough as his attorney, but as his friend... As his friend she'd be setting herself up for a devastating fall. "Does it matter?"

His gaze heated. "Yes."

Somehow, she stayed standing. For an attorney reputed for crafting articulate opening statements and persuasive closing arguments, she didn't know how to tell this man why she couldn't be his friend.

"Eric," she said in her best courtroom voice, "you came to me looking for an attorney." For ten years he'd never called, never sent a Christmas card. "I think we should leave it at that."

Had to leave it at that.

His expression darkened. He swore softly and pulled back. "I can find an attorney in the Yellow Pages."

But he couldn't find a friend.

Not for the first time, Leigh wondered what his life had been like after the phone call that changed everything. One phone call. That was all it had taken. There was a hard edge to him now that hadn't been there before, a bitterness she didn't understand.

"You don't need a phone book," she said, lifting her chin. Being near him sliced her heart into razor-thin ribbons, but she wasn't about to tuck tail and run. She was a grown woman. She could handle this. No way was she letting him stroll back into her life, only to walk back out within twenty-four hours.

He'd done that before.

"You were right to contact me." Passion bubbled inside her as it always did at the start of a case. "I know you. I know you're innocent, and so help me God, I'll move heaven and earth before I let you take the fall for a crime you didn't commit."

Before she'd let her son's father go to prison.

Eric's gaze hardened. "I don't want to force you."

"No one forces me," she said automatically, telling herself there was no way he was referring to that bitterly cold night so long ago. The one for which he'd apologized. "I make my own decisions. I know what I'm doing." She had her eyes open, her heart guarded. She knew the risks, the inevitable outcome. But from the moment Jake had called, she'd known there was no way she could leave Eric twisting in the wind. "Right now I'd really like you to get in the car and let me take you home before this heat does us both in."

A slow smile touched his lips. "I see you still like being in charge."

Her return smile was automatic. "Some things never change."

But others, she knew too well, did.

"I always loved that about you," Eric said, then slid into the car and closed the door.

They didn't speak during the brief drive to Lincoln Park. Words seemed neither necessary nor appropriate. Instead they rode in silence, to the sound of the straining air conditioner and soft blues.

Leigh turned onto Clark and smiled at a group of a boys playing baseball in a park. Connor not only loved baseball, but he excelled as a shortstop. His summer league team had made the playoffs. Their first game was Saturday. Her mother had rushed over the night before, as soon as Leigh had called, insisting she take Connor for a few days. He loved visiting his Gran, after all, and, her mother had wisely pointed out, Leigh needed a few days to get her bearings on this important case. She'd take Connor home with her, have him back in time for his playoff game.

Warmth spread through Leigh as she thought of her mother. She barely remembered her father, just fleeting images of anger and shouting, bitter arguments and drunken tirades. Her parents had split before her seventh birthday. It had been a blessing, actually. Two parents may have been the standard, but if the man and woman didn't love each other and want to be a family, then a child was better off without them.

Her mother had dedicated her life to Leigh, becoming in many ways her best friend. When a twenty-year-old Leigh had tearfully confided that she was pregnant from a one-night stand that never should have happened, Nancy Montgomery had neither judged nor lectured; she'd simply taken her daughter into her arms and held her, promised her everything would be okay.

And it had been. They'd moved to England, where Leigh had won a scholarship to Oxford. The ensuing years had been difficult, but together, Leigh and her mother had managed.

"Take the next left," Eric said, prompting Leigh to abandon the trail of memories.

"Not a good idea," she said the second she caught sight of the army of reporters camped outside the brownstone halfway down the street. News vans blocked traffic. "I'm guessing that's your place?"

Eric swore softly. "Damn vultures. We'll park a few streets over. I can use the back entrance."

She did as he instructed, easing onto a quiet street several blocks down and into a spot along the curb.

"I'll call you this afternoon and let you know our next steps." She shifted the car into Park then reached into the back seat, grabbing the St. Louis Cardinals cap, just in case. "You might need this."

His hand came down not on the baseball cap, but around the backs of her fingers. "You're exhausted and haven't eaten in hours," he said. "Let me fix you lunch." He paused, prompting her to turn toward him. Mistake. There was a warm glow to his eyes, and it penetrated her defenses as effectively as a phone call had once shattered her dreams.

"I still make a mean omelet," he said.

The memory hit broadside, of the night she'd fallen asleep at his place studying, only to awaken to the smell of bacon frying and coffee brewing.

"Thanks, but I'd better not." She didn't need Eric Jones cooking for her. She didn't need to go inside his apartment and see personal artifacts of his life. That was too intimate. It was already uncomfortable enough that they'd spent the night together.

At the police station.

"I need to get home and shower, then head in to the office," she added. She needed to be away from Eric, to breathe.

"Don't run, Leigh," he said in that low, commanding voice of his. "Not from me. Not now."

"Run?" The word left a bitter taste in her mouth. Scared little girls ran. "I'm not running," she said, though deep inside she had to wonder. "I'm building your defense, and that starts with getting back to my office and filing several motions."

"You've barely looked me in the eye. You think I don't know why?"

The air conditioner blew at full blast, but the cold air didn't make a dent in the tension that thickened with every minute they spent cooped up in the front seat of her car.

Slowly, she lifted her gaze to his. "I can look at you." But, God, staring into those piercing blue eyes hurt. Memories and dreams flooded back with a force that staggered. "I just don't think it's a good idea to rush things. We need to focus on your case right now, nothing else."

"I'd rather focus on you."

The breath stalled in her throat. "Eric—"

"How about a walk? That's harmless, isn't it?" He pulled the baseball cap low on his head, hiding his hair but not the hard light in his eyes. "Fresh air might do us both good."

He made it sound so tempting, which she knew was his intent. Eric Jones had always been phenomenal at coming up with the right argument to sway her. At least outside she might be able to breathe without drawing the scent of him deep, deep inside her.

Fighting a smile, she glanced at the quaint street, lined by century-old brownstones, a scatter of parked cars and even an old Harley, trees that provided shade, and felt the ridiculous blade of longing slice clear to her bone.

"Just a few minutes." With luck, nobody would recognize him. "But I'm warning you," she added, trying to lighten the tension. "If I start to melt—"

"I won't let you melt."

Her heart stumbled on the word. He might not have a choice.

"You always wanted to live in Lincoln Park," she said as they headed down the street a few minutes later. While at the University of Chicago, they'd frequented pubs in the area, and often, after late nights of pool, they'd wandered the sidewalks of Lincoln Park, pointing out architectural details and spinning dreams.

For Eric, at least, some of those dreams had come true.

"What's your place like?" she asked.

"Nothing fancy. Four stories, red brick, balconies and high ceilings." He grinned. "I bought the top floor. It was a real fixer-upper, but it suits me."

"It sounds great." Just what he'd dreamed of.

"Thank you."

She ignored the husky edge to his voice. "You're welcome."

"No," he said, stopping suddenly. He reached for her hand and closed it in his. "Thank you for last night, for coming down to the station and standing by me. For believing in me."

Deep inside her, something started to hum. "You don't need to thank me."

"Yeah," he said quietly. "I do. This may be your job, but it's my life and it means a hell of a lot to me that you didn't turn away."

She could never turn away from this man. That had always been the problem. Even when she'd found out he already had a girl back home, a girl he'd known for almost his whole life, she'd still been unable to cut him out of her thoughts. She'd settled for friendship, an easy camaraderie that made her heart bleed every time he smiled at her, touched her, and she knew, deep, deep inside, that the dreams she couldn't chase away would never come true.

Ten years had passed since then, but nothing had changed. Beyond a shadow of a doubt she knew he'd be turning away from her once more, and no matter how much she fortified herself against the blow, her heart would shatter all over again.

Not even that had been enough to stop her from rolling out of bed in the middle of the night and racing downtown.

"It's more than just a job," she said honestly.

And he smiled. "Of all the times I imagined seeing you again, this wasn't exactly what I had in mind."

Leigh's heart took a long, slow free fall through her chest. He'd thought about her. He'd imagined seeing her again. The knowledge jarred her in ways she'd thought she was long since past. "Life can take strange twists and turns. I gave up a long time ago trying to predict what tomorrow might hold."

Many times, she'd learned, she was better off not knowing. It was easier to enjoy the moment without the cloud of heartbreak looming on the horizon.

Eric shook his head. "Damn, it's good to see you," he said in that warm, intimate voice of his. His eyes crinkled. "Do you have any idea how good you look?"

She laughed. "I think we're both living, breathing ads for sleep deprivation," she said, noting that while he still wore the white button-down and gray trousers from the day before, they were no longer pressed and crisp, but wrinkled, almost tired. His eyes were shadowed, the whiskers on his jaw darkening by the minute. "You, my dear Indy, look like hell."

Indy.

She hadn't uttered the familiar nickname in ten long years, had barely held herself together when her son asked if they could buy a copy of *Raiders of the Lost Ark,* his new favorite movie. The guys had bestowed on Eric the nickname of Indy in deference to the fact he was from Indiana and like the hero in the movie his last name was Jones. Indiana Jones.

Indy.

Eric laughed. "I thought women went wild for the scruffy, five-o'clock-shadow look."

She swatted at him. "That's what men like to think."

They started walking again, but Eric did not release her hand. Her heart stuttered and stammered and raced to keep up with the dizzying change, the sudden shift from awkwardness to familiarity. That was the way it had always been between them.

Except for one cold morning.

"How have you been?" he asked. "How's life treated you?"

"Great," she answered automatically, realizing she spoke the truth. Connor was the greatest gift she'd ever been given.

"And your mom?"

"As spry as ever," Leigh said. "We had a wonderful time exploring Europe. We'd probably still be in London if Aunt Louise—her sister—hadn't gotten sick."

A low sound broke from Eric's throat. "Well, that explains that."

"What explains what?"

"Why I couldn't find your mother either."

The comment stopped her cold. "You were looking for my mom?"

Eric squeezed her hand. "When I couldn't find you, I figured she'd be my best source. But I couldn't find a trace of her either."

The breath backed up in her throat, her heart beating so hard it hurt.

"Jake had an address," he went on, "but you weren't there anymore and there wasn't forwarding information. I knew you'd been engaged to some Brit, so I figured you must have married him and changed your name."

They walked slowly, but Leigh could barely take it all in. "Things...didn't work out," she said softly. Trevor had been a prince of a man and he'd adored Connor, but after two years, he'd realized he couldn't settle for only a portion of Leigh's heart.

Eric stopped abruptly. "Goddamn it!"

The vicious curse jumped through Leigh like a live wire. She glanced up at Eric, not understanding his intense reaction to the news of her broken engagement. But he wasn't looking at her. He was looking beyond her, his face a cold mask of fury.

And Leigh knew. They'd been spotted. Ready for battle, she spun around.

But found no one. Nothing looked out of the ordinary, just a bicycle parked on the sidewalk next to a red newspaper stand.

She saw the picture sprawled across the front page of the World Inquisitor, that of a grim-faced, handcuffed Eric being hustled from a squad car and toward the police station.

Then she saw the headline.

Genetic Freaks: Is He One Of Them?

Four

Fury pounded through Eric. The edges of his vision blurred. "Son of a bitch," he swore again, shoving his hand into his pocket for quarters.

"Oh, my God," Leigh said quietly, stepping closer.

Eric shoved the coins into the tiny slot and yanked open the newspaper stand. He pulled out the entire stack of papers, not giving a damn about rules or regulations. This was his life splashed across the front page, a distorted tapestry of lies.

"What happened to innocent until proven guilty?" he demanded, skimming the filthy article. Not only did the reporter already have Eric tried and convicted of the World Bank heist, but this M. H. Cantrell insinuated there might be more to Eric's motivation than greed and corruption.

"This is blasphemy." Leigh leaned against him and stared at the tabloid. "Genetic engineering? A freak of nature?"

Eric ripped off the front page and wadded the paper into a ball, hurled it to the ground. "Someone's going to fry for this."

"Yes, they will," Leigh said in that soft, amazingly strong voice of hers. "But to make that happen, we need to know what we're dealing with." She stooped and retrieved the distorted ball of paper, then smoothed it open.

"Good God," she breathed. "They think you're part of that Proteus mess."

Anger and incredulity twisted through Eric. Several months before, a former low-level CIA operative had gone public with a wild tale of genetic engineering, murder and international espionage. The source claimed that back in the 1960s, the government had sponsored genetic experimentation with the goal of creating a superior race of humans. Some were to have extraordinary intelligence, others extraordinary strength. There was talk about designing babies, being able to designate whether a child was to be an athlete or a scholar. And of course, these superior designer babies would be free of any genetic flaw, virtually erasing the occurrence of disease.

Code Proteus, the effort had been called.

Eric called it ridiculous.

The press called it a gold mine.

In the ensuing months, media coverage had boiled into a feeding frenzy. The original story broke in *The Washington Post,* but from there, the tale had spread like wildfire, edging out Hollywood heartache and political sex scandals in the grocery-store tabloids. Reporters had set out in search of learning the outcomes of the project called Code Proteus. Anonymous so-called government sources claimed the experiments had been a success, to some degree. Children had been born with special skills, though no one knew how many births had occurred. Some accounts said five. Another story alleged six. Still another claimed the number was well over ten.

No one knew for sure. The majority of the government files had turned up missing.

Somewhere along the line, something had gone hideously wrong with Code Proteus. The lead scientist had been murdered, a source claimed, the children kidnapped by those who sought to use their superiority for evil. Allegedly the children had been rescued, sent into hiding. But not before their memories had been erased.

Rumor had it the children were still out there, adults now, living, breathing time bombs somewhere in their mid-thirties. News reports claimed the missing children had grown up in adoptive families, with no awareness of their sordid background, superior strengths or potential for chaos.

The reporter who'd been leading the charge, M. H. Cantrell, implied that Eric was one of the missing children, that he'd used his superior intelligence to steal billions.

Leigh looked up at Eric, stricken. "This is crazy."

"He's making me out to be some kind of superhuman freak just because I was adopted."

A small smile pushed aside the horror in Leigh's gaze. "I don't know, Eric, I've always thought you were pretty extraordinary."

"Not when it comes to computers." He didn't even come close to possessing the know-how to pull off a sophisticated, intricate crime like hacking into the World Bank.

Light twinkled in her eyes. "So maybe my defense should center around proving you're just not that smart?"

God help him, he laughed. His freedom, his future, hinged on proving he was just an average, ordinary guy. "Eric Jones, too dumb to steal hundreds of billions of dollars from the World Bank."

This time, she laughed. "Might not be so good for business, though."

"Going to prison wouldn't be any better."

That sobered them good and quick. "My God," Eric

said, shoving a hand through his hair. He hadn't thought the situation could get any worse, but Cantrell's article would add fuel to the fire.

And make it more difficult to get a fair trial.

"I want this retracted," he said abruptly. "How the hell can we expect jurors to forget garbage like this?"

"You'd be surprised how many people don't pay attention to the news," Leigh pointed out.

"This is hard to ignore."

"We can seek a retraction, but I doubt that will do any good. Our best shot is going for a change of venue."

"Let's do it, then."

"Or..." Leigh hesitated, chewing on her lip. "Eric, have you ever looked for your birth parents?"

The question zinged in from nowhere and stopped him cold. "No."

"That's another angle," she said. "If can prove you're not connected to Code Proteus, that will take away one form of ammunition."

"No." The word came out hard and automatic. He hadn't been given up for adoption as a baby. His mother hadn't been a scared teenage girl. Whoever she was, she'd kept him for two years before deciding she didn't want him anymore.

Eric didn't remember her, didn't want to. He didn't remember the orphanage where she'd left him. The Joneses had adopted him six months later. They were the only parents he'd known.

The only parents he wanted to know.

Leigh touched his arm. "I know this is an emotional subject, but if we have any hope of squashing these ridiculous rumors—"

"I'll take an IQ test."

"Your IQ is through the roof, Eric. We both know that."

True enough. Never, however, had Eric imagined he'd regret that fact. "Then we'll come up with something else. We'll focus on the theft itself, prove the evidence was planted."

Leigh sighed. "You're not betraying your adoptive parents by looking for your birth parents."

"I know that," he bit out. He just didn't want to thrust himself back into the life of the woman who'd made it clear she didn't want him in hers. "This isn't about who gave birth to me. That's just a smokescreen someone's trying to create to distract everyone from the truth."

"Why you, Eric? Why would someone target you?"

"Because Jake is getting too close and they need to discredit him." He filled her in on everything Jake had revealed about his investigation into the World Bank heist and his brother's kidnapping, the attempt on his life. "With me under arrest, Jake loses credibility. The government will believe his attempts to steer the investigation in another direction are based on his friendship, not objectivity."

Leigh pushed the hair back from her face. Dark shadows circled her expressive brown eyes, reminding Eric that she was operating on virtually no sleep. "This is crazy."

"Welcome to my life."

Leigh glanced down at the picture of him handcuffed and being led from the squad car. Several seconds later she looked back at him. "There's something else you need to know."

He didn't like the gravity to her voice. "What?"

"When the judge set bail at three million dollars, I

called my banker to see how much available cash I had.''

"You shouldn't have done that," he said automatically.

"Well, I did," Leigh said. "And it seems a wire transfer had just been made for enough money to pay off my mortgage, my car, and send my—" She stopped abruptly, almost violently. Her eyes went dark. "—send my mother on that world tour she's always fantasized about."

Eric just stared at her. "How much?"

"Half a million dollars."

Holy God. Implications twisted hard. "Where the hell did that come from?"

"That's the question," Leigh said.

Eric had heard about that kind of thing before in organized crime cases, where attorneys on the mob's payroll suddenly and inexplicably came into large sums of money. "I had nothing to do with that, Leigh. You have to know that."

He wished he had that kind of money lying around.

Then again, maybe it was a good thing he didn't. The feds would no doubt allege his wealth came from crime, not hard work.

"What I think doesn't matter," Leigh said. "The prosecutor will see this in line with the charges against you. If you stole billions, it should be simple to drop a gift into your attorney's account."

If Eric had stolen three hundred fifty billion dollars, he'd never do something that obvious.

The sun broke through the haze and burned down on them, working its way through the branches of the elm under which they stood. But everything inside Eric felt cold. Horribly, insidiously cold. He, better than most, knew how cruelly one moment could change everything. And it was happening again. One moment, one piece of bad luck. And once again, Leigh was the one standing by his side. He'd never stopped missing her, her warm smile and soft laughter, her quiet intelligence, but good God, he didn't want her back in his life like this. Someone knew his every move. Someone was playing games with him, dark, dangerous games that could cost him his freedom.

He didn't want her involved. He didn't want her hurt.

All his life he'd taken care of others, protected them, worked to keep them out of harm's way. And all his life he'd been the one with the answers. He didn't have those answers now, but he would find them and crush whoever had done this to him, no matter how powerful Jake said they were.

He would not let Leigh get bruised in the process.

"I should never have come to your office yesterday," he said. At the time, he hadn't expected Jake's warning to come true. He'd just been taking a precaution. And he'd wanted to see Leigh. "I don't want you involved with this mess."

Leigh went very still, save for the glitter in her eyes. "It's too late for that," she said, sounding eerily like the girl he remembered *and* the attorney he'd met the day before. "I *am* involved and you're not getting rid of me that easily."

Like he had before.

She didn't say the words, but they cut through him all the same.

"It's too dangerous." Powerful forces were working against him. They'd already created a trail of falsified evidence strong enough to sway the FBI. Instinct warned they were just getting started.

He took her hand and squeezed, looked into her eyes and tried to make her understand. "I could never live with myself if something happened to you."

She stood a little straighter, smiled a little stronger. "I'm not the girl you remember, Eric. I'm not a wilting wallflower. I'm a woman and an attorney and I can take care of myself. I've worked nasty cases before."

Eric frowned, for the first time seeing Leigh Montgomery as the woman she'd become. The echo of the girl she'd been glowed in her eyes, merging with the gutsy, polished attorney in the tailored pantsuit to create a woman he wanted to know a hell of a lot better. The thought of her practicing criminal law, of her interacting daily with dangerous scum made his blood run cold. Protective instincts surged. "How nasty?"

She blinked. "What?"

"You said you've worked nasty cases before. I asked how nasty."

"That doesn't matter," she said dismissively. "I know my way around a courtroom. I can handle whatever someone throws at us."

He lifted a hand and eased the thick dark hair back from her face. "That's not what I meant." The images wouldn't stop. They pounded through him, dark and ugly. Leigh meeting with murderers. Leigh alone in an interrogation cell with a rapist. Leigh putting her life on the line in the name of justice. "The thought of something happening to you twists me up inside."

Her eyes flared wide. She lifted her hand to his, still cupped against her jaw, and stepped closer. "Nothing is going to happen to me, and nothing is going to happen to you. We're going to prove this case against you is malarkey and then life will get back to normal. You have to trust me on that."

Normal. He didn't know what that was anymore. Standing there in the midday sun with Leigh Montgomery gazing up at him through those amazing, calm, reassuring eyes of hers, he knew nothing would ever be normal again. Even if charges were dropped before sunset, he couldn't go back to life as it had been two days before. Everything had changed. He'd found Leigh again. Nothing, not the FBI nor the sinister cowards who wanted him to take a fall, would take this chance from him.

"I don't like it. I don't like it one damn bit." But he also knew how stubborn she was. Now that he'd dragged her into this mess, she wouldn't back down, even if that meant working behind his back. And that was one thing he couldn't allow her to do.

A slow, womanly smile curved her lips. "Don't get any macho ideas, Indy. Have you ever known me to change my mind?"

Very rarely. Only once, actually. "Have you forgotten that stogie I talked you into trying?"

She laughed, swatting his hand from her face. "What choice did I have? You were on your knee and you were begging. It was pathetic. I couldn't let Matt and Ethan find you like that."

So she'd taken his Churchill and put it to her mouth. But instead of just taking a puff, she'd inhaled.

Her subsequent coughing fit had scared Eric half to death.

"Would that still work?" he asked now. "Getting down on my knee and begging?"

He meant the question in jest, but the light drained from her eyes with the abruptness of a sudden power failure. Then came the sheen of moisture. "It's too late for that."

The quiet statement landed like a punch to the gut. Long after they'd said goodbye and she'd driven away, Eric was left wondering just what the hell she'd meant. Too late to remove her from the case?

Or too late to make amends for the past?

He stood in the shadows, watching. Always watching.

"Jones is out on bail," he reported, moments later.

The mobile phone reception crackled, but the hard voice on the other end defied static. "And Ingram?" asked the superior he knew by number and not by name.

Through dark sunglasses, he watched Eric Jones take Leigh Montgomery's hand and practically drag her toward the alley leading to his brownstone. "Still here. Still living under the delusion that he can make a difference."

"He can make a difference. He can lead us straight to the answers we need."

That was the only reason the ridiculously celebrated Texas banker was still free to come and go as he pleased. Ingram's crusade for the truth made him more valuable as a scout than a captive.

"You know what to do next," the man on the phone instructed.

"Yes." Not only did he know, he relished. Opportunities like this didn't come knocking every day. Jake Ingram was a marked man, and those who'd marked him had deep, deep pockets.

"Make it fast. And make it clean."

"Like disinfectant," he said, then brought the call to a close. Anticipation flooded him. He'd grown up in a household where his father worked backbreaking hours for pennies. He'd been a miserable man, living a miserable life. Work came first, he'd taught his only son.

Work defined a man. Work meant they'd always have food on the table.

But food didn't matter when a heart-attack claimed you at the age of thirty-seven.

The old man had been wrong. Dead wrong.

Work didn't just put food on the table. The right work afforded you any table you wanted, in any house you could imagine. And the right work was so much more than a job.

The right work was like making love to a beautiful, willing woman—erotic, creative and undeniably satisfying.

Late-afternoon sun poured through the wall of windows in Leigh's office. She sat at her desk, staring at a grainy photo of Eric shaking hands with a tall, darkly handsome man clad in a white tuxedo. The two looked casual and relaxed, Eric's smile warm and sincere, the other man's pleased. The picture looked like so many others Leigh had in a scrapbook from her college years of Eric and his buddies laughing and cutting up.

Except the man in the photo was not Jake Ingram, Matt Tynan or Ethan Williams. The man in the photo was Nikoli Dusek, eastern European financier and playboy, and alleged emissary for General Bruno De-Bruzkya, the militant leader of Rebelia and suspected benefactor of the World Bank heist. And the blurry photo that had popped up on Internet news sites less than thirty minutes before firmly established a link between Eric and Rebelia.

Not good.

But not all bad, either. The picture gave Leigh another critical piece of the evidence being compiled against Eric. After her fruitless meeting with the federal prosecutor earlier in the afternoon, Leigh knew the ambitious, not-willing-to-budge Rebecca Salinger would have someone's head for leaking the photo to the press.

"It was a cocktail party." Eric leaned over Leigh's massive leather chair, his face so close to hers she didn't dare turn his way. They'd be nose to nose then. Mouth to mouth. As it was, the masculine scent of sandalwood efficiently and effectively slipped through the concentration she tried to hold in place.

"I don't remember who introduced us," he added, "and the man sure as hell didn't tell me his real name. Yuri, I think he said. Yuri Bozk-something."

Leigh minimized her browser and swiveled her chair to the left, allowing her to stand without brushing against Eric. "They've been planning this a while," she said, hoping that if she moved away from her desk, he would follow. She'd put the picture of Connor in a drawer and made sure no notes about PTA meetings or baseball games were lying around, but having Eric in her personal space disturbed her. Better her office, however, than her house. Or his. Homes were too personal, too intimate. And for the foreseeable future, she had to remain as professional and objective as possible.

The time for the personal would come later.

"How long did you and Dusek talk?" she asked.

Eric joined her at the window overlooking Lake Michigan. "Long enough for that picture to be taken."

"Contact since then?"

"None."

Leigh looked out over the impossibly blue lake, instinctively counting the sailboats drifting like toys in a bathtub. The sight normally soothed, but not now. Adrenaline and concern and fatigue jammed inside her like the gnarled traffic below. She hadn't slept in over thirty-six hours. She'd barely had time to eat. To think. Eric Jones was back, God help her, not just in her life, but accused of what the press dubbed the crime of the century. A crime the president had demanded solved as part of his Fight Fear initiative.

"The major networks are calling," Eric said. "They want me on the morning talk shows."

"Not a good idea." Anything he said would be analyzed and scrutinized, twisted and contorted. Cantrell had called, as well, at both her office and Eric's home. He wanted an exclusive, saying he'd give Eric's voice a chance to be heard. "The statement we released this morning will have to satisfy them for now."

Anything else was too risky.

"Then what?"

Steeling herself against the impact of Eric's piercing eyes, she turned toward him. He stood in the wash of late-afternoon sun, looking every bit as rough around the edges as she felt, despite the fact he'd showered and changed into khakis and a black golf shirt. Shadows darkened his normally piercing eyes, whiskers his jaw. The hard lines to his face told her he was working hard to hold anger and frustration in check.

"I'm going for an examining trial," she told Eric, "but Judge Albright is a hard-liner. With a high-profile case like this, he's not likely to cut the defense any slack."

Eric narrowed his eyes. "What does that mean?"

It meant they had a hard road ahead of them. "Other than the search and arrest warrants, we'll have little information about the case against you."

"How can that be legal? I thought they had to disclose the evidence to the defense?"

"Not before the grand jury meets." Grand juries

handcuffed the defense and gave a rubber stamp to the prosecution. "Since this is a federal case, the prosecutor needs a grand jury indictment. I won't be allowed into the proceedings, and typically only minimal evidence is presented, so as not to tip the prosecution's hand. Salinger will only present enough evidence to secure a true bill."

Which grand juries almost always delivered, wrapped up tidily with a ribbon and a bow, like year-round Christmas gifts for the prosecution.

"An examining trial creates an exception," Leigh explained. "An examining trial would allow me to put Venturi on the stand and ask him detailed questions about his investigation and the information that led to your arrest. It's a form of discovery."

"Let's do it, then."

"I'll file the request, but the chances are slim. Examining trials are rare. And, as I said, with the spotlight on this case, Albright is going to play it straight. He's not going to risk presidential scorn."

Eric's expression darkened. "That's bullshit. How the hell do we fight this, if we don't know what they have against me?"

Leigh frowned. The judicial system was designed to protect the innocent, but Eric was right. Many processes and procedures were tipped in favor of the prosecution. And in this case, with a jittery nation looking on and the president hungry for a conviction, the odds were stacked even higher against them. She would fight with everything she had, but deep, deep inside, a cold feeling spread through her, the realization that everything she had might not be enough to keep her son's father from spending the rest of his life in prison.

"Leigh?" Eric put a finger under her chin and tilted her face toward his. His eyes were hot and glowing and they damn near ripped her heart from her chest. "What's wrong?"

Five

She could barely breathe, that was what was wrong. She was a savvy, creative attorney, but when Eric looked at her like that, when he touched her, her brain shut down and sensation took over. Longing washed through her in thick, suffocating waves.

Once, she'd loved this man wholly and completely. She'd never forgotten his voice, his laugh, the warmth that glowed in his eyes. As she stood there so close to him, with his hand to her face and his gaze concentrated fully on her, the desire to feel his arms around her, to feel their bodies pressed together and hear his heart beating, almost knocked her flat.

Forcing a breath, Leigh stepped back from the torture and reminded herself she had to focus. She had to be strong. She could not let Eric Jones or the past distract her, touch her.

"After the grand jury—" she said, using her professional voice to hide the hated breathlessness. But that was all she could manage. What was wrong with her? She wasn't a silly school girl anymore, damn it. She was a grown woman, and this man was part of her past. She tried again. "We'll request typical pretrial information— their list of witnesses and experts, transcripts of police statements and interviews, lists of everything seized and what was found on your computer, that kind of thing."

Eric closed his eyes, opened them a moment later.

Cold certainty glimmered bright. "You think I'll be indicted."

Something deep inside responded to the wariness in his voice. The urge to put a hand to his or, worse, put her arms around him and hold him, just hold him, warred with common sense. He looked so alone standing there, accused of a crime she knew he didn't commit. His life was being turned upside down, and even if—when—she proved him innocent, there would always be those who looked at him with suspicion in their eyes. That was the kicker with the justice system. Innocent until proven guilty sounded well and good, but even when the accused was found innocent, many still saw him as guilty.

The shadow of doubt lingered for a long time.

Eric didn't deserve this. The heartache and disappointment littering their past lost all importance, all relevance, in the face of what lay ahead.

"Better than a seventy-five percent chance," she acknowledged.

He swore softly. "So what do we do?"

The question pulled her from the haze of nostalgia and returned her to the comfort zone of lawyer-client relationship. She crossed the plush rose-colored carpeting to a small round conference table in the opposite corner of her office. There, she had notes spread out and a tablet waiting.

"You tell me everything you know," she said, picking up her pen. "Come sit down."

Eric remained standing stoically at the window. "I can't."

The sudden gust of warmth was ridiculous. Of course, Eric Jones couldn't just sit down and let someone else take over. He'd always been the one in charge, the one to take command of a situation when no one else knew how. This reversal of fortune had to be eating him alive.

"Okay," she said, realizing the futility of arguing. "Just answer a few questions, then."

"Whatever you need to know." He crossed to her, his big body moving with the masculine grace she remembered from so long ago. He'd been lankier then, more boy than man. But during their years apart he'd filled out in all the right places. His shoulders looked broader, his thighs more powerful, and while she didn't think he'd actually grown taller, he dominated a room more fully than he had before.

"You said they took your computer?" she asked.

Eric nodded. "My laptop, as well as all my floppy disks and CDs."

"How do you connect to the Internet?"

"DSL line."

Leigh looked up from her notes. "Damn."

Eric didn't need an explanation. "Open line?"

"Makes it a breeze for anyone who wants to hack into your computer."

"And plant evidence," he supplied.

"Bingo," Leigh said, wishing she could get her hands on the computer, but knowing it was probably tucked away at FBI headquarters in Quantico, Virginia, by now. "The feds obviously found some kind of link between your computer and the World Bank, maybe erased code or other program files."

"There were manuals of some sort," Eric said. "I saw them in evidence bags as they were arresting me."

Leigh jotted notes, already planning her defense. First thing in the morning she'd make phone calls and set her strategy into motion. "What kind of manuals?"

"Looked like computer programming manuals."

"Were they yours?"

"Found in my bedroom, but I'd never seen them before."

Leigh sucked in a sharp breath, let it out a moment later. "Thorough bastards, aren't they?"

Eric leaned against the wall and let his head loll back. "Christ, Leigh, I keep thinking you're going to wake me up and I'm going to realize this is all some weird *Twilight Zone* dream."

Leigh looked away from him, trying not to think about the fact that if she were to wake him, that would mean they'd been sleeping together. "I wish," she said, then cringed deep inside.

She did *not* wish they were sleeping together.

"The good news," she said, standing, "is that so far everything seems circumstantial, which is easier to defend. The standard for conviction is beyond a shadow of a doubt, and it's difficult to reach that level of certainty with nothing concrete. Computers can be tampered with, those manuals were clearly planted, and even that photo of you and Nikoli Dusek doesn't mean a damn thing. Just because you shook the man's hand at a cocktail party doesn't mean you're in bed with him."

A hard sound broke from Eric's throat. "I should hope not."

Despite the gravity of the situation, she smiled. "I meant that figuratively, of course."

A slow smile curved his mouth. "We don't want to give the prosecution another angle to play, after all."

She didn't know how it happened, how Eric managed it, but her smile bubbled into a small laugh. It had always been like that between them, tense moments broken by stupid nonsense. "No, we don't." She rubbed the back of her neck. "We don't have a lick of motivation, either."

Eric pushed away from the wall and crossed to her. "Other than greed, you mean."

"Well, yes, there's always that. But you're a successful businessman, you own your own home, and you—" Her words stopped abruptly when he moved into her personal space and stepped behind her.

"Let me," he said, and before she could step away, before she could so much as breathe, his hands joined hers at the back of her neck.

She went completely still, but he didn't. His hands were big, stronger than she remembered. And when he rubbed them along her neck and down to her shoulders, she thought she might just dissolve into a puddle of pleasure right then and there. Warmth sang through her in an achingly familiar rhythm.

The little moan slipped free before she could stop it.

"You're tense," Eric murmured, as his clever hands jumbled her thoughts. "You need to be careful or you'll give yourself a headache."

The memory hung there between them, of the countless times Eric had gently scolded her for pushing herself to the brink of exhaustion or for internalizing problems. He always said she took life too seriously, that she needed to relax. And he'd always done his best to help her do so.

Even when that meant having her lie on the carpet so he could straddle her hips and work magic with his hands.

The intimacy had always been an excruciating combination of pleasure and torture, much like the sensations now humming from pulse point to pulse point. Her blood thrummed with memory and longing. She'd always known his heart belonged to another. She'd known he saw her only as a friend.

But that hadn't stopped the yearning, the impossible desire to be the one Eric Jones shared his heart and soul and future with. She'd felt like a fraud for calling herself a pal when she wanted so much more, but she'd preferred friendship to not having him in her life at all.

But he was back now, and his talented fingers could still play her body like a song.

It took effort, but Leigh found the strength to step away. "I'm fine," she said, turning to face him. Mistake. The intensity in his eyes was as dangerous as his hands. "You're the one I'm worried about."

"Don't be. I've handled worse."

That got her. She stared at him, wondering once again what his life had been like after he'd returned to Cloverdale. He'd had a father to bury, a mother to console, a fiancée to nurse back to health and a business to salvage. No easy task for a twenty-five-year-old who'd been intent on conquering the world of high finance, starting with a plum job he'd already lined up at a high-powered brokerage firm in Chicago.

"How's your mom holding up? Reporters aren't hounding her yet, are they?"

Eric went very still. "No."

Relief washed through her. She'd only met Susan Jones a time or two, but Leigh remembered her as a kind woman with lively eyes and a warm smile. Her love for her son had been obvious and deep. Leigh hated thinking of Mrs. Jones fending off an army of blood-thirsty reporters.

"That's good," she said. "But you should probably give her a head's up. It won't be long before they show up on her doorstep."

"She's dead, Leigh."

The quiet words stopped her cold. She looked at Eric standing in the fading light of late afternoon, the stark lines to his face and bleakness to his eyes throwing her back in time ten long years, to the bitterly cold night she'd tried to explain to a numb and noncomprehending Eric that his father had been in a terrible car accident, that he hadn't survived. That Eric's fiancée Becky had been in the car with him. That she'd been rushed to a hospital where she was undergoing emergency surgery.

To this day, the look on Eric's face haunted her.

To this day, the sound of his grief ripped her up.

She'd taken him in her arms that night, driven by the need to ease his pain, even though she'd known that was impossible. She wanted to do the same now, to erase that stark look from his eyes, but she forced herself to stand very still. She didn't trust herself to move. She didn't trust herself to touch.

"It was last year," Eric added in a horribly thick voice. "The day after Thanksgiving."

Sorrow swamped her. Leigh had always loved the open affection between Eric and his parents; she'd admired his commitment to spending every holiday at home with them. Especially Thanksgiving. Not even a blizzard had stopped him from traveling home for turkey day, his mother's favorite day of the year, the first holiday she and Eric's father had celebrated after bringing a three-year-old Eric home from the orphanage. He'd always bragged about her turkey and dressing, her special cranberry sauce and pumpkin pie.

"I'm so sorry," Leigh said, meaning the words deep, but knowing they would never be enough.

A reflective smile touched his lips. "She was ready to go. She never got over losing Dad."

"Had she been ill?"

His eyes dimmed even more. "Not technically. Not unless a broken heart counts."

Somehow Leigh bit back the hard sound breaking in her throat. A broken heart definitely counted. "That's so sad."

Eric exhaled roughly, but the tension didn't leave his big body. "She moved in with me after Becky moved out. Osteoporosis had set in by then, but her mind was still sharp and she was as stubborn as ever. She insisted on cooking breakfast every morning, and when I'd sit down, she'd read the newspaper to me."

Leigh smiled, memory washing over her like a fond caress. "My grandparents did that."

Eric's expression remained curiously blank. "So did my folks. Dad read to Mom every morning. They got a kick out of finding typos and bad grammar."

Leigh could see it too well. "They were good people."

Eric wandered closer to the table and picked up an unsharpened pencil. "The day after Thanksgiving," he said, rolling it between his big hands, "I woke up later than usual, close to eight. I was still half asleep when it hit me that I didn't smell coffee or bacon. My heart just about stopped. Because I knew. God, I knew. I was out of the bed and running so fast, running down the hall."

Leigh wrapped her arms around her waist, not even trying to fight the tears welling in her eyes.

"She was still in bed," Eric said in an oddly mechanical voice. "The lamp was on and Dad's picture had been pulled to the edge of the nightstand. And Mom…looked peaceful. I'd swear she was smiling."

"That's beautiful," Leigh whispered, imagining Eric's parents reunited after nearly a decade apart.

Eric snapped the pencil in two. "She never got to be a grandmother," he bit out. "She was so excited when Becky and I were married, waiting, waiting for a grandchild to spoil. But it was just like her and Dad all over again—no children." He dropped the two halves of the pencil to the carpet. "After the divorce…it was like something inside Mom just withered away, too."

And for that, Eric blamed himself, she knew. "It wasn't your fault," Leigh said softly.

The deep blue of his eyes glittered. "I tried, damn it. I tried to make that marriage work. I don't know how it took us six years to discover we didn't love each other, not like—" He broke the words off violently. "Not the way we were supposed to."

Leigh sucked in a jagged breath. She'd known this conversation was coming; she just hadn't thought it would be today. "There's not a right and wrong when it comes to love, Eric. It just is."

"There's a right and wrong when it comes to marriage," he shot back. "It was as if we were actors playing out a stale script that should have been retired a long time ago." He paused, looked up and met Leigh's gaze. "Things had started falling apart before the accident, but after…" He eyed another pencil on her desk, before roughly turning away. "She couldn't walk for almost two years. There was no way I could turn my back on her. I was all she had."

And Eric Jones lived and breathed responsibility. "You two had been together forever," she recalled.

"She always wanted more," Eric said. "I'd hear her in bed at night, crying, but there was never a damn thing I could do." His expression twisted. "By the time we realized it was over, all either of us felt was relief. For years we'd been going through the motions, pretending for the world and my mother, convinced that once we had children the emptiness would go away.'' He paused, frowned. ''That never happened.''

Leigh could hardly breathe. Guilt sliced through her with painful precision. It *had* happened. Eric had fathered a child. A son whose lopsided smile reminded Leigh so much of Eric that her heart hurt just thinking about it.

A son she hadn't bothered to tell him about.

Stricken, Leigh turned away, realizing in a horrible rush the gross injustice she'd done this man, a man she'd once claimed to love with every corner of her heart. She couldn't imagine anyone better suited to being a father. He would never forgive her for the secret she'd kept, but she knew she had to tell him. Not today, not while the FBI had him in their sights. But after she'd cleared his name, then she'd give him his son.

The irony almost choked her. She'd dedicated her life to truth and justice. She advocated that every man, every woman deserved a chance. But she, purveyor of honesty and champion of fairness, had denied Eric everything she espoused. For over ten years she'd kept a life-changing truth buried deep in her heart.

At the time it hadn't seemed like a lie. She'd been young and scared and broken-hearted, and she'd thought she was doing the right thing. Eric had told her he was staying in Cloverdale and marrying Becky, that he was sorry for their night together and hoped she could forget it. He'd encouraged her to go to Oxford and marry an Englishman, just as she'd always said she wanted to do.

Leigh hadn't been able to bear the thought of adding one more responsibility to his plate. He'd already had his mother and Becky to care for, a business to bail out of trouble. And the two of them hadn't exactly been deeply in love. At least he hadn't. Not with her. They'd been friends. Once he'd made it clear he regretted making love, there'd been no way she could add to that regret by informing him he had a child on the way. She knew what it was to have a father who viewed his child as a responsibility, not a joy. She didn't want that for her son or daughter.

So she'd moved to England, and that had been that.

Except now she and Eric were back in Chicago, and he deserved to know the truth. That he was a father. That he had a son.

He deserved to know.

"Shouldn't there be a security guard down here?

Leigh glanced around the parking garage reserved for her firm. Normally Mercedeses and BMWs sat leisurely in row upon row of reserved spots, but at close to eight o'clock, few vehicles remained. Overhead, fluorescent lights hummed, but they didn't provide much light, only enough to reveal shadows and oil spots.

"I'm sure Ed is around somewhere. He monitors two floors."

Eric moved closer, scanning the shadows and crevices that suddenly seemed sinister. The sounds of their footsteps echoed through the concrete cavern. "I don't like the idea of you down here alone."

The protective clip to his voice sent warmth rushing through her, overriding the chill that had settled deep once she'd realized she had to tell him about Connor.

"This is a secure building," she said, depressing the small black button on her key chain and waiting for the double beep of her car. The guards had done an excellent job of keeping the press out. "You don't need to worry."

Eric slid an arm around her waist, drawing her closer. "You're a beautiful woman. You should always have an escort after hours."

Leigh smiled. For years she'd worked hard to be treated as an equal, not a woman, but Eric's concern made her feel achingly feminine. "I'm fine, really. I'm a big girl. I can take care of—"

"Goddamn it," Eric bit out, stopping abruptly.

Leigh's heart started to pound. Hard. Her car sat where she'd left it that afternoon, but during the hours she'd been upstairs, someone had destroyed the gray paint job on the driver's side. Deep gouges streaked horizontally along both the doors.

Eric charged forward, untucking his shirt as he went. At the front of the car he wrapped his hand in the cotton knit fabric and retrieved a note from under the windshield wipers.

Leigh rushed forward, leaning over his shoulder to read the words scrawled in a bold, messy handwriting.

Eric Jones is taking a fall.
If you're not careful, you'll fall with him.

Six

Eric reacted on instinct. He reached for Leigh and tucked her behind him, shielding her between his body and the concrete wall of the parking garage. His hands itched for some kind of weapon, but he knew if an attack came, he would fight with everything he had before he let anyone touch Leigh.

"I know you're out there, you coward," he shouted, scanning the shadowy parking garage. His words echoed insidiously.

"Eric, don't," Leigh said from behind him. "Just let it go."

"Is threatening innocent women how you get off?" he demanded, incensed. Cold fury snaked through him. Someone was after him, he knew that. Someone had targeted him. He could deal with that. But not Leigh. Not Leigh. He'd go to prison for life before he let this filth touch her.

"It's me you want! Come after me, damn it! Not her."

Leigh pushed against him. "Eric, it's okay, really."

He spun toward her. "Okay? You call vandalizing your car and threatening your life okay?"

She put a hand to his arm. "It's just a stupid note. No harm done."

His blood took on a slow, hard boil. "No harm done?" He gestured toward the car. "How do you know there's not more? How do you know they didn't tamper with your brakes or plant a bomb in your ignition system?'' The possibility filled him with a violence he'd never known. ''How do you know if you slide behind that steering wheel, you'll live to see another day?''

The blood drained from her face, but her words came out strong, classic Leigh. ''I think you've watched too many movies.''

The past forty-eight hours exploded through him. ''I've been arrested for a crime I didn't commit, Leigh. The feds ransacked my apartment, took my stuff. Whatever the hell they found, they think it's enough to fry me.'' Instinctively, he scanned the darkened parking garage once more. He could feel someone out there, watching them, waiting, loving the show. But he wasn't about to leave Leigh to go after them.

''The press is dogging me every step, turning my life into a sideshow. They think I'm a genetic freak,'' he added, turning to her. ''The president himself said he was pleased about my arrest.'' He tried to wrestle the anger under control, but it spewed too frenetically. ''So yeah, crucify me for being paranoid or watching too many movies, but I'm not letting you get in that goddamn car.''

Leigh's eyes went wide and dark, her mouth fell open. Beneath the tailored jacket of her pantsuit, her shoulders rose and fell with jagged, irregular breathing. ''Eric, I didn't mean it like that.''

He knew that. God help him, he knew that. She was the last person he should take out his frustration on. ''I know,'' he said, drawing her close and savoring the fresh scent of apples clinging to her glossy hair. Damn, he wished she'd take it down from the severe twist she'd showed up with this afternoon. "I'm sorry," he said roughly. So damn sorry. "I just don't want you hurt."

Leigh leaned against him, shocking him by curling her arms around his waist. "Don't worry about me."

The resignation in her voice twisted deep. It was as though she knew she was going to be hurt, but didn't care. Gruffly, he murmured, "I do worry about you. You're an innocent in all this."

She tipped her face toward his. "So are you."

The certainty glowing in her eyes warmed through him. "You're amazing." And God, how he'd missed this woman. She'd been only a girl the last time he'd seen her, but even then she'd had the rare ability to bring peace to chaos.

The urge to lower his face and feel her soft lips beneath his slammed in from the darkness. He felt himself moving, his body tightening, saw her eyes widen, her lips part. His heart thundered hard, crashing out a dangerous desire he'd worked hard to forget.

But then she was turning away, struggling out of his arms. "We should call the police," she rasped.

Frustration pierced deep. "You're right," he said, but knew the cops couldn't do a damn thing to stop what was coming. Not from the bastards who'd framed him, and not between him and Leigh.

Eric had learned long ago that inevitability had a mind of its own.

"It won't do a damn bit of good, will it, to tell you I don't want you involved?" Once Leigh Montgomery sank her teeth into something, neither hell nor high water would make her give up. Loyalty and tenacity ran through her blood. Courage shone in her eyes.

"I already am involved," she said, lifting a hand to his face. Her smile was both soft and strong. "And I don't scare easily. No matter how bad it gets, I'm not backing down."

God help him, that was what scared him worst of all. No matter how it soothed his soul to see her, hear her voice and feel her touch, he wished he'd never walked into her office.

"You look great," Jake said, pulling Leigh into his arms. She hugged him back, wholly, warmly and without reservation, the exact opposite of how she'd greeted Eric less than forty-eight hours before.

"You're looking pretty good yourself, Sherlock," she said, pulling back to grin up at him. "It's great to see you."

"You, too," Jake said, leaving an arm around her waist but turning toward Eric. "Both of you."

The two men pumped hands before sitting at the dimly lit, out-of-the-way table Jake had requested. At the university they'd hung out at Ranalli's Pizza with such frequency the staff had known them by name, their pizza and beer preferences by heart.

"Mushroom and green pepper?" Jake asked.

Eric took a deep swig of beer. "You know it."

Leigh was smiling now, all traces of the scare in the parking garage either gone or deeply buried. The police had arrived within minutes, Venturi a short while later, and after a thorough inspection of Leigh's car turned up no sabotage, they were allowed to leave. Of course, Venturi had made his skepticism clear. He'd also made it clear that by no means did petty vandalism and a cheap note mean Eric was being framed. Anyone could have staged the scene. Anyone.

Even Eric.

Venturi had let the insinuation hang there between them, before turning to walk away.

"This isn't the first time something like this has happened," Leigh had told the officer. "Defense attorneys aren't exactly on everyone's popularity list."

She'd said the words lightly, in jest, but they chilled Eric to the bone.

Frowning, he looked at Leigh, and felt everything inside him go painfully tight. She looked heart-stoppingly beautiful sitting there with the light of a flickering candle casting a warm glow to her face. On the drive over she'd complained of a headache brewing, prompting him to suggest she take down her hair. And she had. Now the long glossy strands danced around her face and made his fingers itch to reach over and see if the texture would be as silky as before.

"It's official." Jake glanced at two men in dark suits sitting a table away, his bodyguards, then lowered his voice. "The World Bank removed me from the case."

Leigh put down her Corona. "That's ridiculous."

"It's the plan," Eric pointed out, signaling the waitress for another round. It didn't escape his attention that Jake had requested the most secluded table. And that he sat with his back to the wall. "Whoever these bastards are, they're thorough."

"We'll get 'em," Jake said in that faint Texas drawl of his. "It's you I'm concerned about, Indy. How are you holding up?"

Eric bit back all the nasty things that immediately surfaced and focused on the facts. He and Leigh filled Jake in on the day's events, speaking in spurts, ending each other's sentences and trains of thought with an ease and familiarity not even a decade apart had destroyed.

"Can you believe that nonsense?" Leigh reached for

her bottle of beer. "They implied Eric could be pre-programmed from birth to commit crimes."

Jake muttered something under his breath as he put down his beer with a thud. "That might not be as far-fetched as it sounds." He glanced around the restaurant, kept his voice low. "Where there's smoke, there's usually fire."

The waitress appeared before he could elaborate, balancing two large round trays on her hands. Jake and Eric moved their beers to make room, but even after the young woman with pierced eyebrows hurried away, no one reached for the gooey pizza.

"Jake?" Leigh prodded. "What are you talking about? You think *The Inquisitor* could be right? You think Eric could be the result of some wild experiment?"

Laughter and conversation filled the crowded dining area, but the world seemed to quiet. "Government files indicate there really was a Code Proteus," he said in an unusually grave voice. "Children really were born, then placed up for adoption."

A chill slithered through Eric. "And these children... You believe they're dangerous?"

Jake stared at his beer a long time before answering. "There's a school of thought," he said slowly, "that they were subjected to a form of hypnotic brainwashing. It's possible they could lead double lives, functioning as law-abiding citizens most of the time, but under hypnotic influences there's the potential they could commit crimes, but have no conscious memory of it."

Leigh pushed the hair from her face. "They could commit crimes they're not even aware of?"

Which meant Eric *could* be the mastermind behind the World Bank heist. He *could* be Achilles. He *could* be the walking time bomb the paper alleged, a man programmed from childhood to commit crimes.

Jake let out a rough breath. "This is all classified, so whatever gets said here, stays here."

Eric pushed the pizza back. The rich smell of tomato that usually brought fond memories and fired his appetite suddenly left him sick to his stomach. "Agreed."

"Absolutely." Leigh's eyes were intent and focused, the small table candle casting a flickering light to her face.

"There was a case recently about a Navy SEAL assigned to protect the American ambassador to Delmonico from a rumored assassination attempt."

"Samantha Barnes," Leigh supplied.

"That's right."

"I remember reading about that in the paper. There was an attempt, but someone else got shot."

"The SEAL got shot," Jake bit out. "Came damn close to dying."

Eric studied his friend closely, watching the way his normally calm eyes glittered. Jake had one hand on his mug of beer, but it was curled so tightly around the frosty glass that Eric almost expected the container to shatter. "How does this connect with genetic engineering?"

Jake's mouth twisted. "The SEAL assigned to protect her was also the one stalking her. Only he had no idea."

"My God," Leigh said quietly. "That's possible?"

"With mind control, almost anything is possible."

"So you think this Navy SEAL is one of the genetically engineered children?" she asked, suddenly sounding very much like an attorney intent on cross-examination.

"I'm not saying that," Jake hedged. "I'm only saying he was under hypnotic influence. That's the danger."

Horror and disgust twisted through Eric. "You're saying I could steal billions of dollars and not even know it?"

Frowning, Leigh reached for his hand. "Don't say that," she said in that strong, reassuring voice of hers. "Don't think it. You had nothing to do with what happened."

But the evidence said that he did. If the newspapers were to be believed, he could be planning more crimes, preparing to hack into other computer systems. The Pentagon. Air traffic control. Nuclear power plants. They were all vulnerable to Achilles—who could be some heinous alter ego buried deep in Eric's subconscious.

The possibilities chilled.

"It's possible," Jake admitted.

The noose around Eric's neck tightened. "I could have massive computer programming skills that never surfaced in any other area of my life," he muttered, but had a damn hard time believing it.

"Yes."

The lively dining area blurred. Eric looked from Jake's stern face to Leigh's stricken expression, not for the first time in his life wondering just who the hell he was.

Seated in the back of a nondescript black sedan, Jake watched his friends walk away. That was what Eric Jones was. His friend. Not his sibling. The two of them, along with Matt and Ethan, had acted like brothers—the Blues Brothers, the girls in school had dubbed them— but Jake knew deep, deep in his bones that genetics did not bind him to Eric.

His friend's involvement in the World Bank crisis stemmed from a far more sinister and deliberate origin.

Eric had been targeted for the sole purpose of playing mind games with Jake. Of derailing his investigation before he uncovered the bastards responsible for playing Russian roulette with his life and the lives of his brothers and sisters.

And by God, Jake was not going to let them win.

Running a hand through his hair, he turned from where Eric and Leigh had vanished around a corner, thankful the press had not found them. All evening he'd noticed odd looks between the two of them, deep, meaningful glances as though they carried on a conversation in which he hadn't been invited to participate. They'd been like that in grad school, and it had amused Jake deeply. Eric had denied involvement with Leigh beyond friendship, but the guys had always suspected the connection ran deeper.

And now he knew.

Eric had taken Leigh to bed, then returned to Cloverdale and married Becky.

And Leigh had a son, not a single picture of whom she'd ever sent to anyone. He'd assumed the child's father had been a Brit she'd met at Oxford, but now, instinct warned that the truth resided closer to home.

"That shouldn't take long, Ms. Montgomery," the second of two private investigators said. "A couple of days, probably. I'll let you know."

Leigh reached for Glenn Moore's hand and shook it warmly. "You know I appreciate the good work you do."

The older man with thinning gray hair smiled. "And

I appreciate the chance you gave me. I won't let you down.''

Leigh had no doubt of that. If anyone could sniff out the information needed, Moore was the man. She'd met him upon her return from London, a washed-up private investigator who'd been framed to take the heat for a slick, middle-aged con artist. Glenn had been hired for a routine surveillance job, never suspecting his client was seeking cover for a string of thefts in an upscale neighborhood. As jewelry and electronics began disappearing, the residents of the posh subdivision recalled seeing an unfamiliar man sitting in a van, day and night, just watching.

Glenn had been arrested, some of the loot found in his apartment.

He'd come to Brightman and Associates in search of a defense, and while Thomas had displayed little interest in the case, the haze of desperation in Glenn's eyes had tugged at Leigh. She'd taken the case, and, relying on Moore's investigating skills, she'd gathered enough evidence to prove his innocence and send his client to prison.

And in the process, she'd earned a steadfast ally.

After the two said goodbye, she crossed to the wall of windows, scanning the glimmering lake beyond. The sweltering heat had yet to break, very few clouds intruding upon the picturesque blue horizon. Soon, the blistering sun would set on the third day since Eric Jones had walked back into her life.

She'd fought her way through the cluster of reporters camped in the main lobby shortly before seven, intent on setting wheels into motion. She'd barely slept the night before. Too much adrenaline and energy crashed around inside her. Too many memories. Too many consequences. And the house had been unnervingly quiet. She was used to Connor's constant chatter, to the television blaring and video games beeping.

The ache started all over again, tightening her chest. She'd talked to her son the night before and first thing this morning, but she missed him desperately. He was happy as a clam with his grandmother, but Leigh wasn't used to being separated from her child.

The cold certainty of what lay ahead chilled her to the bone.

Connor had first asked about his father when he was two years old. Leigh had been wholly unprepared for the question, but she'd long since decided she would not lie. Instead, she'd told Connor his father was a good man, but he couldn't be with them. Of course, Connor, being two, had wanted to know why, why, why. And for that, Leigh had found no answer.

Over the years, Connor had continued to ask about his father, typically on his birthday and Christmas. He wanted to know if maybe, sometime, his dad might be able to be with them.

The question had always cut deep.

I don't know, sweetie, Leigh would say. Maybe.

How would he react? Leigh wondered now. How would he react to Eric Jones? Would her son accept his father? Would his father accept him?

Would either of them forgive her for stealing nine years from them?

And what would happen if she couldn't prove Eric's innocence? If he went to prison for the next twenty years?

How would she forgive herself for that?

The questions had kept her awake deep into the night, twisting and taunting. Every time she closed her eyes, she saw Eric in the shadows of the parking garage, his big body positioned between her and an unseen assailant, his eyes hot and on fire. She'd never seen him that angry, that…incensed.

Even now, almost twenty-four hours later, the memory of those volatile minutes alarmed her in ways she didn't understand.

Exhaling raggedly, she lifted a hand to the back of her neck and rubbed. She tried not to think about the way Eric had touched her the day before, the warm pleasure he'd sent drifting through her, but breaking into Quantico would have been simpler.

She hadn't talked to him since early afternoon. He'd gone into work today, but his superiors had quietly suggested he leave. His presence, and that of the reporters tailing him, wasn't good for business. Until the trial was over and the shadow of doubt gone, it would be best if he kept a low profile.

Leigh frowned, remembering the frustration in Eric's voice. He'd been unusually gruff, telling her not to worry about him. He knew what he had to do.

So did she.

From the front seat of a drab navy rental car, he watched Leigh Montgomery emerge from the elevator and stride through the dimly lit parking garage toward her car. She paused and glanced around, then lifted her chin and continued with purpose.

That morning her high heels had clicked against the oil-slicked concrete, but at some point during the afternoon she'd changed into a pair of sexy black boots which made little sound.

"She's asking too many questions," his superior had

complained earlier in the day. "I thought you said she was harmless."

Those hadn't been his exact words. "Leave Leigh Montgomery to me." The leggy brunette was tougher than he'd planned, had failed to heed his first warning, but he wasn't finished with her yet. Soon both Jones and the little lady would realize this was a game they could never win.

So would Ingram.

"She won't find anything," he'd promised. No one would. Few would even think to look in the right places. "She's grasping at straws."

"See to it she stops."

Jones Declares Innocence, the front page of the *Chicago Tribune* had read that morning. "My client is a man wrongly accused," Leigh Montgomery had been quoted as saying. He watched her now, sliding into her Camry and closing the door, stealing his view of her lithe body. "He's not Achilles. He's not a criminal. Eric Jones is an innocent man who's been targeted as the fall guy for a crime about which he knows nothing."

Red taillights glowed in the darkness as she backed from her parking space. "I won't rest until his name is clear," she'd vowed in the article.

He slid his car into reverse and followed. She would stop, all right. He would see to that.

And as with every other aspect of his job, he would be creative, and he would enjoy.

With the clock pushing toward ten, Leigh turned onto a narrow, car-lined street south of downtown. Of the eight visible street lamps, light glowed from only one. The majority of the local establishments had shut down, windows boarded up. Halfway down the block a local

tattoo parlor was doing its usual brisk business, while
next door, music and patrons spilled from a beat-up
building that had once been a drugstore.

Not finding a spot on the street, Leigh parked in a
side lot, but didn't immediately turn off the engine. With
the doors still locked, she glanced in the rearview mirror,
confirming one more time that she no longer resembled
a downtown attorney. She'd darkened her makeup and
slicked back her hair, traded a pantsuit for black jeans,
a black scoop-neck T-shirt and a leather jacket. Boots
completed the look.

Satisfied she wouldn't stand out like a debutante in a
prison cell, she reached for her pepper spray and turned
her mobile phone on. She'd been to this part of town
before and had never encountered problems, but she'd
learned the value of precaution.

*You're a beautiful woman. You should always have
an escort after hours.*

The memory slipped in from the darkness and sent
warmth streaking through her. The ache came next. It
wasn't fair. Ten years should have erased the misplaced
draw she'd felt toward Eric Jones. Ten years should have
eradicated the attraction. Ten years should have killed
the longing.

They hadn't. Instead, Leigh was coming to realize that
everything she'd once felt for Eric Jones had merely
been buried, shoved deep, where the pain couldn't hurt
her daily. But with every minute she spent with the man,
old feelings came surging back, not faded or threadbare,
but strong and vibrant.

But still, wholly misplaced.

The second she told Eric about the secret she'd kept
all these years, the grandson his mother had never had

a chance to know, to love, any chance of a future would shrivel up like wildflowers during a drought.

That didn't matter, she told herself. All that mattered now was making sure Eric didn't spend his life in prison. Her objectives were clear. Fight the charges against him. Nail the unseen bastards trying to frighten her. And above all else, resist the attraction that made her body catch fire the second her client walked into a room.

That was how she had to think of him. Her client. Not her former lover, the man to whom she'd given her virginity, and certainly not her son's father. Those labels were too personal, too intimate.

Too devastating.

For now, Eric Jones was just her client.

Yeah, Leigh thought grimly. And the sun was suddenly going to rise and she would awake to realize the past few days had only been a dream.

Frowning, she opened the car door and stepped into the hot, sticky night. Off-key strains of jazz mingled with the el rumbling by, while warm, humid air closed around her like a vise. From a cloudless sky, a full, faintly orange moon shone like an eerie ball of fire.

Please be here, she thought, heading from the rundown lot where only three other cars sat. *Please be here.*

Awareness hit immediately, hit hard. She stopped walking and listened, just listened, instinctively slipping her hand into the front pocket of her tight jeans.

Someone was watching her. She could feel the presence of another just as surely as she felt perspiration breaking out on her body.

Someone was waiting.

Show no fear, Leigh reminded herself. It was just a short distance to the Blue Note; inside she would be safe. The owner, Charlie Mac, knew her. He was a friend of

Glenn Moore's. Once she was inside, he would keep an eye out for her. And when she left, he would walk her to her car.

She had only to get to the club.

Hand curled around the small vial, she started forward. Her boot stepped onto the concrete of the curb, but with unmistaken certainty she heard a faint crunching noise. On impulse she spun around.

She saw no one.

Only shadows blowing in the warm evening breeze.

A cat, she told herself. Maybe a scrap of newspaper skittering down the street.

With renewed confidence she reached the sidewalk and approached the tattoo parlor, not allowing herself to look back. She was safer that way, she'd learned over the years. Never look back. Only forward. Her imagination had a nasty habit of playing tricks on her. Cruel, twisted tricks that made her heart pound so hard and fast she could barely breathe. The vandalism to her car and the cryptic note had obviously rattled her more than she'd realized.

With the Blue Note less than fifty yards away, the tight coil of anxiety loosened. A trio of teenage boys and two giggling girls lounged outside the tattoo joint, while a little farther down the street, two men argued outside the nightclub. She would be fine as soon as she—

She heard the footsteps behind her too late. An arm snaked around her waist and dragged her from the sidewalk, toward the darkened, boarded-up building that had once housed Faye's Diner.

Fight-or-flight kicked in. She slammed an elbow into her attacker's gut and stomped down on his foot, spinning toward him with her pepper spray raised and ready.

Then she went absolutely, completely still.

"Whoa," Eric said, reaching for her wrist. His fingers curled around bone and flesh, as he angled the spray away from his face. "I'm not going to hurt you."

For a moment, Leigh just stared. Then reality shoved aside shock and she came to life. "You idiot!" she shouted, twisting free of his grip. "You scared me half to death."

"How the hell do you think I felt when I saw you driving into this neighborhood?" he shot right back. "You told me you had an errand to run, damn it!"

"This *is* the errand," she practically growled in return. "You followed me?"

The line of his jaw hardened. "I didn't like how vague you were."

"That doesn't give you the right to follow me. Don't you realize what could have happened? I could have hurt you."

"This isn't about me, Leigh," he said, taking the pepper spray from her hand. "This is about you and chances you have no business taking."

"You're my client, Eric, not my chaperone."

He moved so fast she barely had time to absorb what was happening. In a cruel heartbeat he had her crowded up against the side of the old diner, his body blocking out the world beyond. She could feel the heat from his chest and his legs, the rapid thrumming of his heart. And though the night was dark and the shadows deep, nothing hid the fierce glitter in his eyes.

"Your client?" he said, in an ominously quiet voice that pulsed through her blood like a dangerously seductive drug. "Your chaperone? Is that what you think I'm trying to be?"

Leigh didn't know what to think. Not anymore. Not

with Eric Jones standing so close she could feel every hard, hot ridge of his body. Not with him staring down into her eyes with an intensity that made her pulse hum. "Eric," she managed. "Please."

"Please what?"

Step even closer. Never leave. Kiss me. "Let me go."

The lines of his face went even harder. "I can't, damn it," he said pushing closer. "Don't you understand that? I've dragged you into a dangerous game you have no business playing. You could be hurt, and it would be my fault."

Leigh wasn't sure how she stayed standing. If he hadn't been pressed up against her, she might not have. "I'm a grown woman," she told him for the second time in twenty-four hours. "You didn't drag me into anything." She hesitated, met his eyes, felt her body catch fire.

"I'm exactly where I want to be," she said through the sudden thickness in her throat.

Where she'd wanted to be for years.

For a moment Eric just stared at her. Stared hard. Down the street a horn blared and tires screeched, but Leigh couldn't tear her gaze from Eric's. Slowly, those piercing eyes never releasing hers, he lifted a hand to her face and slid his fingers along her cheekbone and into her hair.

"God help us both," he bit out softly, and before Leigh realized his intent, he lowered his mouth to hers.

Seven

He knew it was too soon even as his mouth came down on hers, as he felt her lips part, heard the little gasp tear from her throat. The problem was, knowledge didn't stop him. The need to touch, to taste, burned too deep. Too hot.

For ten years this woman had existed only in memories. For ten years he'd had nothing but hazy impressions from that long-ago night, the welcoming warmth of her mouth, the startling feel of soft flesh pressed to his, the silent tears as they'd come together.

For ten years, he'd tried to convince himself the flare of passion had been the result of emotion running high.

For ten years, he'd fought the truth.

He'd called Leigh Montgomery friend, but somewhere between the early-morning classes and late-night study sessions, between shared pizzas and coffee, between laughter and poker games, a taboo relationship had grown deeper. He'd fought the attraction with everything he had, treating Leigh like a kid sister even when he saw the disappointment flare in her eyes. His future belonged to Becky, he'd known. And even if Becky hadn't needed him so desperately, strict rules existed regarding behavior between grad students and undergrads in the classes they taught. He could have been kicked out of the graduate program if his superiors suspected his relationship with Leigh extended beyond friendship.

But they'd never suspected. For a long time not even Eric had suspected. Not until that night when boundaries shattered, lives along with them.

"Leigh," he murmured against her open mouth, drowning in the feel of her, the taste of desire and wintergreen. Everywhere her hands skimmed, his body burned. With excruciating clarity he remembered the feel of her warm and naked, running her hands along his back and buttocks, curling her legs around his thighs.

And again, he wanted.

He wanted Leigh Montgomery. The truth burned through him now with an intensity that almost sent him to his knees. Ten years ago responsibility and protocol had stood between them, but those barriers didn't exist now.

He wanted to kiss her everywhere, to skim his mouth along her jawbone and her neck, lower still to her chest, to pull a nipple into his mouth and taste the breasts he could feel pressed against him. Instead, he pulled back and cradled her face, needing to see her, just see her, to convince himself she was real and not some cruel figment of his imagination. She gazed back at him, glossy hair long and tangled around her face, her smoky eyes wide and slightly glassy, her mouth moist and swollen from his kiss.

"Leigh," he murmured again. "I'm not going to let anything bad happen to you."

He wasn't going to let anyone or anything steal the second chance they'd been given.

Her eyes flared for the briefest of seconds, before she pulled him back against her. This time the kiss was hers. She was the one who claimed his mouth, who threaded her hands through his short hair and held him in place, who opened for him, acted as though she wanted to drink him in. "Eric," she whispered, sliding a hand through his hair. "Eric."

A groan broke from his throat. He pressed closer against her, angling his knee between her thighs. She wore tight dark jeans, but the fabric couldn't conceal the heat of her body. The second he slipped through, she closed her legs around his, cradling him intimately against her body.

Eric almost lost it right then and there.

He moved his knee against her in a steady rhythm, running his hands from her face and down her neck, to the swell of her breasts. Her nipples had been a beautiful soft pink, he remembered vividly, and when he'd danced his tongue around them, they'd grown darker, firmer. She'd arched into his mouth, much as she was now arching into his hand, eager and demanding.

"You're amazing," he murmured, slipping a hand to her waistband. He wanted flesh, damn it. He needed to feel the warm softness of her skin. "You're the most amazing woman I've ever known," he added, sliding his mouth to sprinkle little kisses to her cheekbone. "I'm not letting you go again." He was rocking against her now, loving the feel of her thighs closed against his knee, of her breast filling his hand.

Except she'd quit responding. It took a second for reality to pierce the haze of desire. Her hands no longer tangled in his hair. Her legs no longer clamped his. Even the sounds of her ragged breathing had gone completely quiet.

"Leigh?" Eric asked, pulling back.

She stared at him through dull, shocky eyes. Her cheeks were no longer flushed, but pale.

"Leigh?" Hammering through him was the need to lift a hand to her face, to touch her gently, slowly, as he should have done all along. But he didn't let himself move. "Are you okay?"

"No," she whispered, drawing a hand to her mouth. "No." She twisted away from him then, staggered out of the shadowed doorway and into the night. "This is wrong."

Her broken words cut through him, but nowhere near as much as the stricken look on her face.

"No it's not," he said with a gentleness at excruciating odds with the ferocity pounding through him. His body was hot and hard and on fire, but intensity wasn't what Leigh needed. He'd hurt her badly. She had every right to be leery of him. "There's always been something between us, Leigh. Always. You know that as well as I do."

A sad smile touched the mouth he'd possessed so thoroughly only moments before. The mouth he wanted to possess again. "Yes, there has," she admitted. "And it's always been forbidden."

Not what he wanted to hear. "It's not now."

Moisture flooded her eyes. "Yes, it is."

"You've said it yourself," he reminded, trying to keep his voice low and reassuring. He understood her reluctance, deserved it, knew it was a defense mechanism. But he'd also felt the welcoming warmth of her body, the way she'd rocked against his knee. "You're a grown woman. You make your own decisions." He paused, stepped closer. "And I'm a grown man. There's no denying we want each other." Not after the way they'd practically made love right there in the darkened doorway of an old diner. "We're both unattached—"

Sweet mercy. It hit him then. Leigh didn't wear a ring, but that didn't mean some lucky bastard hadn't cemented his place in her life. Her bed.

"Is that it?" he asked roughly, hating the sudden gust of cold that chilled him to the bone, the realization that he might be too late. When Leigh went home tonight, she could be giving herself to another man, while Eric lay hot and wanting and alone in his empty bed. "Is there someone else, Leigh?"

She swiped at the single tear that spilled over her lashes. "I wish it was that simple," she whispered. "There's so much you don't know."

"Then tell me," he urged, lifting a hand to trail his fingers along her neck.

Something hot and hurting flashed through her eyes. "Please, don't touch me," she said with a hitch to her voice he'd never heard. "It's wrong."

"No, sweetheart, it's not. It's so damn right I can barely see straight." Barely think, barely breathe.

"You're my client," she said, and though her voice was still raspy, the words came out strong. Her eyes took on a dark glitter, and when she lifted her chin and smoothed the hair from her face, he literally saw the conversion from woman to attorney. "Getting involved on a personal level breaks every rule in the book." She glanced down and pulled her leather jacket closed over her untucked scoop-neck top, hiding the swell of her breasts. "The taboos are still there."

"But they don't have to be," he pointed out. "They won't always be."

"You don't know that," she countered, "and neither do I. All I know for sure is that until this case is over, no matter how tempting it is, no matter how badly I wish things were different, I can't let loose ends from the past override my objectivity."

"Can you do that, Leigh?" he asked roughly. God

knew he couldn't, not when it came to this woman. "Can you be objective?"

The question landed at Leigh's feet with the force of a hand grenade. She looked at Eric standing mere inches from her, the hard demand in his eyes and the strong set to his jaw, the firm line to the mouth she'd kissed so desperately only minutes before. He no longer had her pressed against the door of the old diner, but his body blocked the warm breeze blowing in from the street, leaving her to feel only him. Breathe in only him. See only him.

Just like always.

No. She couldn't be objective. Not when it came to this man. She couldn't treat him as if he were Jake or Matt or Ethan. She couldn't make believe she hadn't lain in bed more nights than she cared to remember, burning from the memory of his touch. She couldn't ignore the fact she'd given him her heart and her body, that she'd made love to him in her dreams with such a powerful intensity she'd sometimes awakened with her body screaming from the aftermath.

She couldn't pretend she hadn't given birth to his son.

"Leigh?" His voice was softer now, gentler, seeping through defenses she'd mustered every ounce of strength to tack up between them. "Talk to me."

"I have to be objective," she said, as much to him as to herself. If she let her heart override her head, he could go to prison, and Connor would never know his father.

Eric's expression gentled, but he didn't move a muscle, kept his big body entirely too close, making it painfully obvious his desire had yet to fade.

He streaked a finger down the side of her face. "Are you telling me if you weren't my attorney, you wouldn't have pulled away? You'd have let me take you back to my apartment?''

The breath stalled in her throat. If he'd kissed her one second longer, if he'd touched her breast, she would have gone up in flames. They would never have made it back to his place.

"Leigh?" He tucked his finger under her chin and tilted her face toward his. "Is this because of before?"

The question pierced with unerring precision, and before Leigh could stop the reaction, she felt herself wince. He wanted an answer, deserved one, but she had none to offer. Her refusal to take their relationship to another level had to do with before and now and times yet to come.

It had to do with the truth that wove through her chest like a vine tightening around her heart.

It had to do with the fact that soon this man would hate her, and it would kill her to let him back into her heart, her body, only to have him walk away from her.

Again.

Eric let out a rough breath, but rather than pulling away as she expected, wanted, he braced his forehead against hers. "I've never forgiven myself for what I did to you that night," he rasped. "I've replayed every minute, every mistake, over and over in my mind, wondering how I could have been such a bastard."

His words, the truth she knew lay behind them, punished in ways she'd never learned how to defend. She knew he meant them sincerely. She believed him when he said he'd relived the hours they'd made love. So had she. But whereas her memories had been tender and aching, his had been fueled by regret.

"You weren't a bastard," she said softly, smiling to hide the pain.

"The hell I wasn't." He stepped her back to the wall of the diner, caging her in by bracing his hands against the old brick wall. "You're the last person in the world I wanted to hurt, but that's exactly what I did."

"I don't want your guilt, Eric." Didn't want to see the regret glimmering in his eyes. "That night was a long time ago," she said softly. "Life goes on."

That was both the problem and the blessing.

His eyes met hers. "And how has your life been, Leigh? Would you change anything if you could?"

Oh, yes. She'd change a lot. Not the fact that she'd made love with Eric and conceived his child, but the fact that he'd never seen her as more than a friend, that he'd walked out the door and never come back.

"I can't change anything," she said. "That's just it. And neither can you. Ten years is a long time. People change." She'd made the best decisions she could, even if retrospect cast them into question. "There are things you don't know about me, Eric, things that could change everything."

"I highly doubt that."

Tell him, some voice deep inside whispered. *Tell him now.*

But she couldn't. Not tonight, not while a prison sentence hung over his head like an executioner's noose.

"When you look at me," she said with a soft smile, "you see the girl from before, but I'm not her anymore. She stopped existing a long time ago."

The night she'd given her heart and her soul, her body, to Eric Jones, only to have him marry another.

Warmth glimmered in his eyes, and the slow smile curving his lips looked far more genuine than the forced gesture she'd given him. "No, Leigh," he said slowly, softly, gently, "when I look at you, I see a beautiful,

intelligent, courageous woman I'd like to know a hell of
a lot better.''

Oh, God. The longing, the need, to slip her arms
around his waist and return her mouth to his screamed
louder, harder. Because when she looked at him, she saw
the boy she'd once loved with all her heart and a man
she longed to know more intimately. But she also saw
a client accused of a crime with far-reaching consequences.

And above all else, she saw her son's father.

"Time, Eric. We have to give it time."

"I might not have time," he ground out, the words
punching through her defenses clear to her heart. "Unless a miracle happens, I could be spending the next
twenty years in prison."

No. That wasn't going to happen. That was why she
had to stay objective. Eric Jones might spend the rest of
his life hating her, but she would never let him get sent
up the river for a crime he hadn't committed.

"You need to have a little more faith in me," she said
with a smile she didn't come close to feeling.

Eric's mouth twisted. "Faith and I aren't exactly on
good terms right now."

"Well, that's going to have to change," she told him,
forcing herself to forget the past and the future and con-
centrate only on the now. The case.

"We're going to fight the charges against you, and
we're going to win." And then, God help her, the real
trial would come. "No matter what the newspapers say,
the evidence against you is circumstantial, and that can
be refuted. That's why I'm here." She pushed the hair
from her face. "The only way to outsmart a hacker is
through another hacker."

Eric narrowed his eyes. "Another hacker?"

Already she felt stronger, more in control. "We may not have your computer, but the FBI can't do a damn thing about the cyber trails," she explained. "Someone has tampered with my checking account, with your savings account, with the entire World Bank," she said. "And despite how smart Achilles is rumored to be, he's bound to have left a trail, no matter how faint."

"A trail the FBI missed?"

"A trail they had no reason to look for after the evidence against you appeared." She paused, hooked her arm in his. "A trail we're going to find."

Eric followed when she started walking. "How?"

"A kid named Hack," she explained. "Henry Crance. He's called Hack because he makes slipping in and out of computer systems look like child's play."

Which to him, of course, it was.

"We find Hack," she said, "and we find your trail."

They didn't find Hack. At least, not in the run-down blues club south of downtown where he typically hung out. They waited for hours before giving up and leaving word for him to call.

Shortly after three the next afternoon, he did.

"He's all over it," she told Eric that evening, following a late-afternoon court appearance. As expected, the judge had denied her request for an examining trial. "He's going to snoop around the World Bank computer systems and see what he can find."

Eric turned from the wall of windows at the far side of her office. He'd been standing there for close to twenty minutes, listening to Leigh explain the court proceedings as the sun sank on yet another day. "He's that good?"

"He's the best," Leigh answered without reservation. "It's scary what that kid can do."

Eric shook his head. "Watch Achilles turn out to be some pimply-faced thirteen-year-old punk in his daddy's basement in Des Moines."

Wasn't that the truth. "Stranger things have happened."

Like Eric Jones being labeled a criminal mastermind.

He strode toward the mini bar at the far corner of her office. "Thirsty?"

"No, thanks."

He poured a glass of mineral water, then turned toward her. "You mentioned a few other trails he's going to look into?"

"What he really wanted is your laptop, but it's safe and sound in Quantico now."

"Safe and sound my ass. The FBI wants to nail me. I hardly see them looking for echo cyber trails when the president is breathing down their neck and I'm a ready-made target."

He was right about that. Sending the computer to Quantico was like inviting the prosecutor to authenticate evidence. "What about Matt or Ethan? Don't they have contacts all over the place?"

Eric grinned. "One day you'll cast a ballot for Matt Tynan as president, and he'll appoint Ethan Williams as his director of the CIA."

The tension and fatigue Leigh had been battling all day drained away, replaced by an anticipation she hadn't felt in a long time. "I can see it." Ethan had always been vague about what he did for a living, never refuting the international playboy label the magazines had bequeathed him years ago. But Leigh would bet her last dollar there was more to their pal than met the eye.

If anyone had contacts in the FBI, secure contacts who could give Eric's computer a fair inspection, Leigh was putting her money on the dynamic duo of Williams and Tynan.

"Have you talked to them lately?"

Eric finished off the water in one deep gulp. "Not in a few months. They both left voice mails after the arrest, but..." He paused, frowned. "What the hell am I supposed to say to them?"

"Nothing," Leigh said. "They know you're innocent. I'm sure they were calling to lend their support."

Just as they'd given their support after Eric's father had been killed. Leigh had called them after she and Eric had received that horrible phone call, and the guys had probably broken the land speed record getting across campus. They'd stayed for hours, Jake trying to secure airline reservations, while the rest of them rallied around Eric. He'd been numb, in shock, trying valiantly to put on a tough face. He was the buttoned-up one, after all. He was the problem solver, the one who always knew how to wiggle them out of whatever jam they got themselves into.

Eric Jones hadn't known how to be the one in need, just as he didn't know how to be that man now. He didn't know how to ask for help. How to accept it.

Good thing Leigh had never allowed Eric's stubbornness to sway her.

"How about dinner?" she asked. "I'm exhausted and can't bear the thought of facing my stove."

Eric looked up from where he'd been rolling the empty glass between his big hands. "Sounds great. How about Chez Paul's? Or if you'd rather Italian, Harry Carry's can't be beat."

The thought made her mouth water, but she had other

plans for Eric Jones. "I don't know," she murmured, making a production of glancing at her watch. "I'm not in the mood for crowds." Reporters followed them ruthlessly. Crowds gathered. People stopped and stared, pointed.

But exposure wasn't the only reason Leigh didn't want to dine in public.

Frowning, she glanced around her office. "I've had all of these three walls and a window I can stand for one day. How about your place?"

Eric just stared at her. "You want to go back to my place?"

She heard the surprise in his voice, saw the pleasure glow in his eyes. And for a moment, a blade of guilt nicked at the swirl of heat. After the explosion of passion the night before, she knew her suggestion sounded like a complete reversal, but she needed him at his place and dinner seemed the best smokescreen.

"We could order pizza," she suggested, even though they'd eaten at Ranalli's a few night before. "Maybe Chinese. And then we can take care of a few loose ends."

Eric's eyes took on a slow, hot burn. "What loose ends?"

The question seared through her every bit as much as his touch had the night before. She'd lain awake for hours, reliving every skim of his fingers, every caress, wondering how she'd found the strength to resist him.

It had been so achingly long.

She'd lost herself last night, lost herself as she'd not done in ten long years. She'd forgotten about everything that stood between them, the lies and the heartache, the court case and their son. Everything had been swept away by the intense longing to feel his arms around her, his mouth on hers, his hard body pressed deliciously close.

The truth burned, damned, terrified. She'd thought this man out of her life, her blood. Now she realized she'd only learned to ignore the longing that had nearly shredded her so long ago. The emotion had survived, strengthened while it lay dormant and the girl became a woman, the boy a man. And it was more dangerous now than before.

She forced her thoughts back to his question. He wanted to know what loose ends. "About the day you were arrested," she forced herself to say. *Not* the way they'd mauled each other the night before. "I want to give Hack as much information as possible."

He held her gaze, didn't look the least bit convinced. "Gotcha."

Oh, and he did. He always had, from the first day of class in her freshman year, when she'd dragged into the auditorium at seven-thirty fully prepared to be bored out of her mind, only to see Eric Jones standing near the podium in a crisp white shirt and khaki pants, his eyes crinkling as he grinned at something a cute young blonde had said to him.

From then on, she'd been lost.

Still was.

"Mr. Jones, when are you going to break your silence?"

"No comment," Eric barked, muscling his way through the crowd of reporters camped outside the front door of his brownstone. He held Leigh's hand in his.

"Just a short statement, that's all we want."

"What does the FBI have against you?"

He pushed a key in the knob and turned, ushered

Leigh inside before the media circus could spill in behind them.

"It's a damn zoo," he growled.

"They'll get bored soon enough," Leigh predicted, "and move on to something else."

He muttered something unrepeatable under his breath. The other tenants of the building had been amazingly supportive, but he knew their patience had to be wearing thin. His was. The media and the FBI were following him everywhere. His whole life was on display under a freaking microscope.

They took the three flights of stairs leading to his apartment in silence. At his door, Eric slid the key into the deadbolt, but didn't turn the lock. Her hand still in his, Leigh stood by his side in the shadowy hallway. She wanted to go inside with him. For the first time since he'd walked back into her life, she was willing to go inside his home. To be alone with him.

After last night, the thought had his body burning with an anticipation completely out of proportion with the situation. She was his attorney, he her client. She'd made those lines starkly clear.

They were dining in because she was tired, and though she hadn't said the words, Eric knew she hated the way people pointed at him and whispered, stared with revulsion.

That was why they were here, he reminded himself. That was the only reason.

But as he turned to her and saw anticipation glowing in her eyes, the way her mouth was slightly parted and her long, silky hair was blowing in the warm breeze, logic crumbled.

He'd always thought her a stunner, but while the guys had raved about her long legs, Eric had been partial to her eyes. Long-lashed and heavy-lidded, the soft brown had glimmered with a thirst for life he'd always admired. Always wanted to save just for himself.

She had that same look to her now, a soul-shattering combination of courage and vulnerability, dread and determination. It was as though the thought of walking into his apartment alarmed her, as though she knew her life could change before she exited again, but classic, gutsy Leigh, she absolutely refused to back down.

And he hated it. He'd made it clear he'd like to take their relationship to the next level, but he didn't want her afraid of him, of them. He didn't want her going inside his apartment unless she was every bit as ready as he was.

"Leigh." He slid the hair from her face and let his fingers linger against her cheekbone. "You're sure about this?"

Her eyes flared wide, an emotion he didn't understand streaking through those deep-brown depths. But when she spoke, she sounded strong and sure. "I'm here, aren't I?"

He slid his thumb toward her mouth and gently rubbed her lower lip. "That was you and me last night," he reminded her. The memory had his body catching fire all over again. "If we'd been here and not standing on some run-down street, we'd have ended up in bed."

This time he recognized the emotion in her gaze, the shock and the vulnerability, the longing and the regret. They swirled deep, mixing with a sheen of moisture he'd rarely seen from Leigh. She smiled softly, sadly, lifting a hand to lower his from her face.

"I didn't come here to make love with you, Eric," she said, her voice quieter than before.

But sooner or later, it was going to happen. Too many

lingering ends dangled between them, too many unexplored and unresolved feelings.

"At least you call it making love and not having sex," he said with a smile he hoped would ease the anxiety making her stand there so rigidly.

Leigh put a hand to the door and slowly let out a raspy breath. "Eric, I don't want to lead you on—"

"You're not," he said, cutting her off. "You've made it clear how you'd like our relationship to be." The way she'd kissed him last night had shattered any question he'd had. "We can take it slow if you need to, as slow as you want." He wasn't going to jump her bones or force her. "You just need to know I'm not going to hurt you. I'm not going to hurt you ever, ever again."

Her eyes met his, and in them, he saw an uncertainty that cut to the bone. "I need a glass of water," she said in a voice suddenly thick. "It's burning up out here."

It wouldn't be any cooler inside, not with the two of them in the same room. But Eric had just promised to take things slow, so he didn't point out the obvious. Instead he held her gaze a long moment before turning from her and opening the door, letting her into his world.

"Home sweet home," Eric said, closing the door behind her.

She stepped ahead of him and looked around, forcing Eric to see his home, his life, through her eyes. The foyer opened into a spartan main room, dominated by male essentials—a big-screen TV, a state-of-the art stereo system, a leather sofa and the obscenely comfortable recliner he'd bought to commemorate his divorce. The walls were white and bare, save for two old-time framed prints of Wrigley Field hung opposite the TV. He hadn't realized Leigh would be coming over tonight, so he'd not taken time to straighten the magazines and books on the battered wood trunk that served as a coffee table, but at least he didn't have fast-food bags or beer cans lying around. The ceilings were high as he preferred, with thick white crown molding circling the room. And the curtainless windows Becky would have hated let the lengthening shadows of early evening spill across the hardwood floor.

"It's wonderful," Leigh said softly, moving deeper into the room. She glanced toward the kitchen and smiled. "It suits you."

What suited him was seeing her here, with a light in her eyes and a smile on her face, in his home.

"Make yourself comfortable," he invited, gesturing toward the sofa. "You sure you only want water? I picked up a killer cabernet a few weeks ago—"

"Actually I recommend the eighteen-year-old Glen Morangie," came a voice from behind him.

Eric spun around on a blast of hot adrenaline, primed and ready to attack.

The sight greeting him stopped him cold.

Eight

There were three of them, tall, big men with purpose glinting in their eyes. They weren't rough-hewn and dirty thugs, but casual and relaxed as they strolled from Eric's kitchen as though they owned the place.

"It's about time you got here." With short dark hair and gleaming eyes, Matt Tynan looked about ten years too young to be one of the most influential presidential advisers to take Washington by storm in recent memory. "We were beginning to think we'd have to start without you."

Ethan Williams grinned. "Don't worry, though, Indy," he said, sauntering closer and thumping Eric on the back. As always, he had his shirtsleeves rolled up, deck shoes on his sock-less feet. "We made ourselves comfortable while we waited."

Jake shoved a glass tumbler in Eric's hand. "Sure beats the cheap stuff you used to keep on hand in grad school."

Eric just stood there. Shock gave way to surprise, surprise to a levity he hadn't felt in too long. Once, they'd been inseparable, the four of them. Once, they'd been able to laugh away, shrug away, wink away anything. They'd been boys then, even if they'd thought they were men. Life had taught them otherwise, beginning the night Eric's father died. In the ensuing years life had jettisoned them down different paths—Matt into politics and Ethan into some secretive international world he refused to talk about, Jake into high finance—but the friendship that bound them together had never faded.

Eric grinned. "You ever stop to think I was saving the Morangie for a special occasion?"

Ethan shrugged. "Of course we did. We're here now, so no more waiting."

Matt picked up a stack of mail from the glass table Eric occasionally used for meals and thumped down a deck of cards. "You can pay the gas company later, Indy. Tonight you're going to lose your shirt instead."

Eric watched his friends swarming around his apartment as if not a day had passed since their biggest problems had been studying for exams or deciding which girl to ask to the party Friday night, and felt the noose around his neck loosen.

"In your dreams," he said, taking the envelopes from Matt and moving them to a small table behind the sofa. And he knew. He knew the reason Leigh had been acting so jittery, the origin of the light in her eyes, the one he'd attributed to sexual desire.

Slowly, he turned to find her standing by the couch, watching them with a smile so pure, so bright, his heart almost stopped. "This is why you wanted to come back to my place."

I'm not here to make love with you, Eric.

She lifted her chin. "Hope you're not disappointed."

If only she had any idea. He closed the distance between them and before she could step away, turn away, cupped the back of her head and kissed her full on the lips. In front of everyone. She might not have come here to go to bed with him, but she'd given him a gift all the same. A gift only she could have known the value of.

"Impossible," he said, pulling back to give her a smile.

Leigh Montgomery could never disappoint him.

But she could surprise him. The woman who met every battle head-on, who'd earned the reputation of a barracuda in the courtroom, looked away abruptly. Eric wanted to turn her face back toward his, to see if that really was uncertainty he'd caught in her eyes, but then Jake was there, kissing her cheek, sliding an arm around her waist.

"She grew up good, didn't she?" he said, glancing toward the guys.

Eric forced himself to look from the sight of his friend's hand on Leigh's body, reminded himself almost violently that he had no real claim to her and that this was Jake. His friend. The man who'd warned him of the charges gathering against him, who'd directed him back to Leigh in the first place.

"She's always been perfect," Eric muttered.

Leigh met his gaze for a long heartbeat, then glanced at Matt and Ethan, but they were grinning and cutting up, completely unaware of the private conversation between the two of them.

"Do I get a kiss, too?" Ethan asked.

Matt slugged him. "You're a married man now, 007," he reminded, angling toward Leigh's face.

Ethan didn't acknowledge the innuendo about the secret life he vehemently denied, but did give Tynan a good shove. "This from the lovesick puppy who's called his fiancée three times since leaving for the airport. What's the matter? Afraid she'll finally see through those Tynan moves and change her mind?"

Smiling, Leigh hugged each man. "Thank you for coming."

"Anytime," Matt said with a playful wink. "I've been waiting a long time to bail the Boy Scout out of trouble."

"I hear you need a little help with the FBI," Ethan added with the devilish twinkle in his eyes that had helped earn the four of them the dubious distinction of Blues Brothers. He slid a Cuban cigar from his shirt pocket and handed it to Eric. "I might have a friend or two who can help out."

"One of your nameless, faceless friends who don't really exist?" Matt asked.

Ethan only shrugged.

"Pizza should be here any minute," Jake added.

"And then Indy's going down," Ethan promised. "I haven't forgotten those four hundred quarters you swindled from me last time." He pulled out a lighter and lit a cigar for each man. "It's time to pay the piper."

"I love you, too, Con. You just keep being a good boy for Grandma and I'll see you in a couple of days."

"You'll be at the game Saturday?"

"I wouldn't miss it for the world."

"Cool."

A few minutes later Leigh turned off her mobile phone and pressed it to her heart. She stood on Eric's patio, overlooking the quiet street below. A breeze blew in from Lake Michigan, but the air remained warm and sticky, classic August in Chicago. Soon, though, cooler temps would prevail.

At least as far as the weather was concerned.

I didn't come here to make love with you, Eric.

His smile had been slow, hot. *At least you call it making love and not having sex.*

Even now, long hours later, Leigh wasn't sure how

she'd stayed standing, didn't know how he could reduce her to a jumble of nerves. Didn't know how he could ignite the ache with only a few words.

But it wasn't just words, and that was the problem. It was how their bodies reached for each other, the lingering loose ends that wanted so badly to be tied. Make love, have sex, go to bed, the label didn't matter. The intent, the outcome, was the same.

Resisting Eric Jones the cocksure grad student had been hard, but resisting the fully grown man, the man with simmering blue eyes and a rock-solid body, who spoke in no uncertain terms about what he wanted, who said words she would have given anything to hear ten years before, promised to be her undoing.

Exhaling raggedly, she glanced through the sliding glass door toward the table where the four men were laughing, no doubt at one of Matt's wild White House tales or one of Ethan's countless "innocent" adventures. Seeing them together filled Leigh with a warmth and sense of rightness she hadn't felt in too long. It was like clicking the pieces of a puzzle together and discovering perfection.

Fighting emotion, she turned to the night and slid down against the brick wall, next to a clay pot of red geraniums. She'd tried to leave as soon as the pizza arrived, but the four of them had literally blocked the door. Then Ethan had found and hidden her car keys. She was staying, they said. Period, end of story. And so she had.

For a couple of hours she'd relaxed in Eric's recliner, watching the Cubs get trounced by the Astros while listening to the guffaws of male laughter as they puffed their cigars. The smoke had sent nostalgia wafting through her, unearthing a longing so strong she'd been forced to come outside and call her son. God, she missed him. Since the day he'd been born she'd barely been apart from him longer than twenty-four hours. He was her heart and her soul, a gift she thanked God for on a daily basis. When she came home from a grueling day in court, all it took was the sight of Connor's crooked smile to send the ugliness slipping to the background.

Mom, what's my dad like?

He's like you, Con. Smart and loyal, good-hearted, strong, and one heck of a shortstop.

Leigh's chest tightened and tears burned the backs of her eyes. She had to tell him. Tell them. She knew that. But dear God she had no idea how they'd react, couldn't stand the thought of the love in Connor's eyes and the heat in Eric's vanishing forever.

"How you holding up?"

Leigh looked up to find Jake towering over her. She hadn't even heard the glass door slide open. "Fine," she said, starting to stand, but he hunkered down beside her and slid an arm around her shoulders.

"Needed some fresh air?" he asked.

She glanced at her mobile phone, still clenched in her right hand. "Something like that."

A gust of male laughter burst from inside, mixing with the strains of blues from a pub down the street. And again, Leigh smiled. Aside from Eric, she'd been closest to Jake. She'd always suspected he realized her feelings for Eric ran deeper than mere friendship, but he'd never called her on it.

For a moment she was tempted to lean her head against Jake's shoulder, as she'd done so many times in college. He'd been the big brother she'd never had, with an easy, undemanding way she'd always found incredibly comforting. Amazing that so many years could race by, full of twists and turns, but at the end of the day, friends always found their way back together.

"I hope you're not angry with me," Jake said.

She looked up at him, surprised by the concern glowing in his eyes. "Angry at you? What on earth for?"

He hesitated before answering. "Sending Eric to you."

Leigh went very still for just a heartbeat before releasing a slow breath and letting her head loll against Jake's arm. "You did the right thing."

He searched her face, as though looking for something other than the words she'd given him. "Leigh, about your son…"

"Yes," she said, her heart breaking into a staccato rhythm. It had only been a matter of time. Jake knew she had a child, a child she'd sworn him to secrecy about. She'd just never told him why. "Yes," she said again, and before she could prevent it, her eyes filled.

He didn't hesitate. He pulled her to him, held her to his side. "Ah, Leigh," he said in a low, hurting voice. "I'm sorry."

She angled her face toward his, not caring about the tears that suddenly wanted to spill over her lashes. She was tired of being strong, of keeping everything bottled up inside.

"I didn't know how to tell him," she said, not even trying to hide the way her voice broke on the words. "I couldn't bring myself to ruin his life."

Jake lifted a hand to wipe the tears from beneath her eyes. "You could never ruin Eric's life."

Oh, but she could. Soon, she would. "Don't tell him," she said. "Please. Not yet."

His eyes met hers. "It's not my place," he said simply, and his meaning rang clear. It was hers.

"When this nightmare is over…" She paused, wrestled emotion under control. "When the charges are dropped and Eric has his future back, then I'll find a way to tell him."

"Tell me what?"

Leigh's heart flat-out stopped. She looked toward the door to see Eric towering over them both, a glass of water in his hand and a question in his unusually hard eyes.

"Leigh?" he asked, stepping into the darkness. "Are you crying?"

Shock drilled through her. Words jammed in her throat.

"What the hell is going on out here?" he demanded.

"It's not the end of the world," Jake said, pushing to his feet and offering Leigh a hand. "I'm sure Tara and I will work things out," he said to her as she stood, a look of pure male frustration twisting his features. Then, with a grin to Eric, he said, "Apparently our Leigh is still a sucker for a good romance."

Leigh caught on quickly and playfully punched him in the arm. "Call her when you get home tonight," she instructed. Relief washed through her. "Tell her you're sorry."

A strange expression wiped the glimmer from Jake's eyes. "I wish it was that simple."

What had started out good-humored shifted suddenly, and Leigh sensed something else going on. Something deeper. Something that troubled Jake greatly.

"Sometimes an apology is all we have to offer," she said quietly, ignoring the twist in her own heart. "We can't change the past, no matter how much we wish we could."

He let out a ragged little breath. "It's the future I'm worried about."

Her breathing hitched. Some inevitabilities, after all, *were* etched in stone. Some roads, once started down, could never be turned from. The truth always found a way.

Eric stared for a long, tenuous moment at Leigh, then glanced toward his friend. "Things still rough with Tara?"

Jake shoved a hand through his hair. "She was hoping since I've been removed from the World Bank investigation that I'd go home and we could set a date for the wedding." His mouth twisted. "She doesn't understand that I can't just walk away from this, not when so much is hanging on the line."

"Then she must not know you as well as we do," Leigh said. With deep certainty, she sensed something very wrong in Jake Ingram's world, but had to wonder just how much of the uncharacteristic tension about him had to do with the woman he'd asked to be his wife. "If she did, she'd know you're not a man to turn your back on your friends."

Jake's expression turned thoughtful, but before he could speak, Matt and Ethan strolled onto the patio.

"I told you they were wimping out on us," Matt said, with the same playful smile that had sent coeds swooning in college. "What's the matter, girls? Couldn't take the heat? Afraid I'd get the shirts off your backs next?"

The question hung in the warm night air, for a moment neither Eric nor Jake saying a word. Then they both broke into laughter.

"Looks like Tynan's selective memory is flaring up again," Eric commented to Jake.

"Either that," Jake answered easily, "or he can't hold his liquor the way he used to."

"Yeah, yeah," Matt said. "That's why the two of you left the kitchen, because *I* can't hold my liquor."

"Nah," Eric said. "We left the kitchen because it was downright embarrassing listening to you two lovebirds moon on about Kelly and Carey. It was starting to feel more like a bridge party than a poker game."

Leigh choked back a laugh. She listened to the banter among the guys, the easy camaraderie that had not skipped a beat since college, and felt warmth spread through her. They'd gone their separate ways, but the friendship among the four ran as deep as ever. They were laughing now, Matt and Ethan catching heat for being complete saps when it came to the women in their lives.

The longing swirled in from nowhere, tightening her throat and robbing her of breath, but Leigh refused to let it settle anywhere near her heart. Tonight was Eric's night, and this rich masculine laughter, the warm glow to his blue, blue eyes, was why she'd arranged the last-minute poker game. Matt and Jake and Ethan could give him something she couldn't, and when the smoke cleared and Eric no longer stood accused of the crime of the century, the guys would still be here for him, friends who'd always stood by him, never lied, never kept secrets.

"Next time," Ethan vowed. "Next time you're going down."

Standing in his open doorway, Eric laughed. Ethan Williams had been vowing to beat him at poker for over ten years. It hadn't happened yet. "Keep dreaming, 007."

"Leigh's out like a light," Matt said, joining them. Ethan's flight plan called for a seven-thirty departure, less than five hours away. "I didn't have the heart to wake her. Give her a kiss for me, will you?"

Eric glanced toward the patio, where Leigh had stayed after the guys went back inside for another round of cards. The last he'd seen her, she'd been stretched out on a chaise lounge, staring into the night.

They needed to talk. He'd heard enough of her conversation with Jake to know she didn't fully trust him, that she could confide in Jake in ways she could no longer confide in Eric. And that truth scraped.

She'd been crying, damn it. Crying. Because of him. That truth scraped even worse.

"I wish I'd never dragged her into this mess," he said, frowning. "She's taking risks she has no business taking."

"And that surprises you?" Ethan asked. "Runway was never short on guts."

Runway. Eric hadn't heard Leigh referred to as Runway in ten long years, not since the night he'd exploded at his friends, demanding that they not speak to him of her. Runway had been Ethan and Matt's special name for her, in deference to her outrageously long legs, legs they claimed were more suited to a super model than a coed.

"It's not safe," Eric told them. "She's already been threatened." He told them about the vandalism to her car, the threatening note on her windshield. "If those bastards lay one hand on her, so help me God, the next time I go to jail, I *will* be guilty, and it won't be of theft."

"That's not going to happen," Jake vowed quietly.

"I'll make some calls first thing in the morning,"

Ethan added, "and make sure your laptop gets a fair shake."

"Me, too," Matt added. "There might be a few strings I can pull, a few favors I can call in."

Eric just shook his head. Federal charges hung over his head and the government was breathing down his back, the press was hot on his trail and a prison sentence lurked in his future, but he felt like the luckiest damn fool in the world. He had the three best friends a man could ask for, and the most amazing woman he'd ever known was sleeping on his patio.

She came awake slowly, lulled from the dream by the enticing aroma of sandalwood. She stretched languidly and let her eyes drift open, felt herself yawn. At first the darkness was absolute, until she shifted and saw the glow coming from a sliding glass door. Then she saw the figure standing in the shadows, more silhouette than man.

Her heart kicked, hard, and all at once the hazy blur of sleep crumbled. The evening came back to her on a rush, the wonderful sound of masculine laughter and the achingly familiar scent of Cuban cigars, the awkward moments on the patio, when Eric had found her crying in Jake's arms. A little blade of panic sliced deep when she realized she'd fallen asleep.

"Eric?" His name barely came out more than a sleep-thickened whisper. She drank in the sight of him standing there watching her, his piercing eyes concentrated solely on her, a sheen of gold whiskers making her itch to put her fingers to his jaw. The olive shirt he'd worn to her office had long since gone soft and wrinkly, but somewhere during the night he'd rolled up the sleeves to reveal his forearms. Faded jeans hugged his long legs. "What time is it?"

A slow smile curved his lips. "After two thirty." He stepped from the shadows and sat on the side of her chair. "I didn't mean to wake you."

Her pulse hummed dizzily, a dangerous testimony to the uncomfortable intimacy weaving between them. He loomed over her, making her acutely aware that in less than a heartbeat he could be stretched out alongside her, his body pressed to hers.

We can take it slow if you need to, as slow as you want.

The thought of taking it slow with Eric Jones made her blood sing a song she'd tried valiantly to forget. Tried, but failed. Abruptly, she swung her legs to the side of the chaise and pushed into a sitting position.

"Where is everyone?" she asked, glancing toward the door that led inside.

"Gone." Before she realized his intent, he leaned in and put his mouth to her cheek. "That's from Matt," he said, then shifted to her forehead. "Ethan." Without hesitating, he trailed his mouth down to the tip of her nose. "And that's from Jake."

The breath stalled in her throat, but somehow she forced herself to pull back and make light of the fact that she could barely breathe. "You know how many girls in school would have run naked down the street for a kiss from the four of you?"

She realized her mistake too late.

"That was only three," Eric pointed out, as she'd known he would, then went on to honor her comment. He leaned closer, putting one hand to her waist and sliding the fingers of his other hand into her loose hair. This time he pressed his lips not to her cheek or her forehead or the tip of her nose, but to her mouth. The kiss, *his kiss,* was soft and slow and laced by the lingering taste of Scotch, not filled with the almost violent urgency of the night before, but with a warmth and tenderness that changed the pounding of her heart to an intoxicating strum.

Warmth spread through her like a mind-numbing elixir, bringing with it the dangerous urge to move her mouth against his, to lift a hand to his face and urge him down on the chaise with her, over her, to tangle her legs around his and pick up where they'd left off last night.

"Eric…" She couldn't fight him much longer, especially when he offered his own healing blend of tenderness and passion. She couldn't fight the draw, the longing to let those loose ends find their way back together and to indulge the feelings and desires she and Eric had left unexplored ten years before.

But then he was gone, leaving his hands on her body but pulling back so that their eyes met. His were dark and glittering, not with a boy's passion, but a man's desire.

"And that one?" Leigh heard herself asking, though she barely recognized the husky rasp as her own voice.

He skimmed his thumb along her cheekbone. "Mine."

Leave, something deep inside her demanded. *Before it's too late.* The sane, rational part of her knew she should pull back and walk out the door, get into her car and drive far away, but she could no more move than she could change the events that had set them on this collision course so long ago.

"Do you kiss all your attorneys?" she asked with a brevity she didn't come close to feeling.

He gave her another of those slow, heated smiles he

had down to a dangerous art form. "No, just the ones who arrange secret poker games."

"I see." *Leave*, she told herself again, but instead sat there, staring at him as though not a day, not a betrayal, stood between them. There was only the thick night air and the hypnotic drone of crickets, the sound of their own fractured breathing.

"I looked for you."

The quiet words shattered the spell, slamming into Leigh with near-brute force. She knew what he meant, knew he spoke of what happened a decade ago. "You told me to go."

Eric shifted on the chaise, moving to straddle the chair so that he bracketed her between his body and the back of the chair.

"I never stopped thinking about you," he told her, and his voice was low, thick. "You didn't deserve what happened."

Leigh felt her heart slow, her lungs constrict. Deep inside, walls she'd hammered relentlessly into place started to crumble. She didn't want to hear this. She didn't want to know.

"Eric, don't." She edged closer to the side of the chair, desperate to move out from between his spread thighs. "Please. Let's not go back." She didn't want to open those doors, not yet. Not while his future hung in the balance. "It was a long time ago. We were friends," she tried to explain. "You were in need. I reached out and it happened."

She paused, searching for her attorney's voice, the one that was strong and sure, not softened by sleep and desire. "I cared about you." No point in denying the truth. "Cared a lot. I *wanted* to be there."

He smiled faintly and reached for her hand, threaded

his fingers through hers. "I wanted you there, too," he ground out. "I needed you like I've never needed anyone."

The revelation ripped her up in ways she hadn't known possible.

"Damn it, Leigh," he said roughly, "you need to know I didn't sleep with you that night, then never think of you again. I wanted you to be okay. I wanted you to have the life you'd always dreamed of."

Her throat tightened. "I wanted the same for you."

He closed his eyes, opened them a moment later. "I just thank God I didn't get you pregnant," he practically growled, and her heart slammed against her ribs. "I used to worry about that, worry that one day you'd call and tell me you were carrying my child."

The pain crashed in from all directions, sharp and hard and punishing. Shock winded her. She heard the horror in Eric's voice, the relief that his fears had not come to pass.

Would that have been so bad? part of her ached to ask, but her voice refused to honor the question.

"I didn't call," she whispered. Hadn't known how to.

A bittersweet smile lit Eric's face. "And I didn't think it was fair to call you, no matter how badly I wanted to, not while I was married to Becky."

"You never lied about your intentions to marry her," Leigh reminded him. Eric had told her all about the fatherless little girl who'd moved in next door when he was five years old, the friendship that had turned from puppy love to the first blush of romance. Leigh had listened quietly, her heart silently breaking, wondering if Becky realized she was the luckiest girl in the world. "You never pretended we were anything more than friends."

Eric's mouth tightened. "And in doing so I lied to everyone," he said, and the words sounded torn from somewhere deep inside him, somewhere dark and anguished. "I never realized that what Becky and I shared wasn't close to what it took to make a marriage work."

Leigh couldn't help it. The need to touch, to comfort, was too great. With a soft smile she curved her free hand around the back of his and gently squeezed. "I'm sorry."

In so many ways, for so many things, decisions and choices, secrets and lies, what lay behind and what still lay ahead.

Eric pulled his hand from hers and lifted it to her face. "I missed you, Leigh. All these years, your smile and your intelligence, your courage and your determination…but I couldn't find you."

The fact that he'd looked did cruel things to her heart.

"It ripped me up thinking about you gone from my life forever, married to someone else."

On a deep breath, she met Eric's gaze. "That didn't happen." Couldn't have, not when she looked at her son every morning and saw the man who still dominated entirely too much of her heart.

"I'm sorry," Eric said.

Leigh didn't hesitate. "I'm not."

He moved so suddenly she didn't have time to brace herself, to turn away. Before her heart could beat, his mouth was skimming hers. "I'm glad."

Something inside her shifted. "Eric—"

"I know," he said, pulling back before she could pull him closer. "Slow." His smile had more of a look of pain than of pleasure, but he shifted on the chaise, lifting a leg from the side and easing back so that he lay stretched out beside her. Then he extended his arm and held out his hand.

"Lie with me," he said. "I promise I won't kiss you again unless you want me to. Unless you ask."

Her heart was beating so crazily she was sure he could hear the erratic rhythm. "You sound pretty sure of yourself," she commented, desperately fighting the desire to forget about consequences and accept his invitation, to feel the hard contours of his body hugging hers.

A faint light glowed in his eyes. "Some risks are worth the reward."

"It's late, Eric. I should go."

"Just a few minutes."

Leigh was a smart woman. She knew better than to make memories with this man. She knew better than to open herself up to the hurt all over again. But at that moment, all the knowledge in the world couldn't have stopped her from taking his hand and sinking against his body, feeling her legs brush his, her breasts pressed to his abdomen, her head against his chest, where his heart thrummed as crazily as hers.

Memories were a mistake, she told herself as she sighed in contentment. Memories were dangerous.

"Leigh?"

The raspy tenor of his voice drifted through her, prompting her to tilt her face toward his, where she found him watching her, just watching, eyes dark and focused as he ran his fingers through her hair.

I won't kiss you again unless you want me to.

She wanted. God help her, that was the problem. When it came to Eric Jones, she'd always, always wanted.

Nine

Leigh blinked against the wash of morning light and felt her heart start to pound. Memories—or was it a dream?—tumbled hard and fast, of Eric's mouth on hers, him picking her up and carrying her inside, putting her down on his big, big bed. He'd promised to take it slow, and as she'd lain pressed to his body, feeling his hand skim along her side, she'd imagined what it would be like to go slow with Eric. To stretch every sensation to the breaking point. To turn one moment into forever.

Startled, she sat abruptly.

But this was not her bed.

It was Eric's.

Uneasy, she slid from sheets that carried the scent of sandalwood he always wore, and quickly found her shoes.

She could not have slept in Eric Jones's bed. She could not have spent the night at his brownstone. She could not have made more memories with this man, no matter how badly her heart and body burned to do just that.

The aroma of coffee escorted her down the hall. She wanted to slip away without saying a word to him, but knew that was the coward's way out. She would politely thank him for his kindness the night before, then tell him she had to leave, go home and shower, get back downtown for a few important meetings.

In the kitchen she found a mug sitting in front of an

automatic coffeepot and a carton of eggs on the counter. A slab of bacon sat on a chopping block, adjacent to an onion and two tomatoes. A frying pan waited on the stove.

Uncertainty pushed a little deeper, no longer because she'd slept in Eric's bed, but because of the unnatural stillness to the apartment. "Eric?" She turned toward the breakfast area, where the newspaper lay on the glass top table where the guys had played cards the night before. "Eric?"

Nothing.

Her heart started to pound, well-honed instincts kicking hard. Clearly, Eric had been here not that long ago, in the middle of preparing breakfast.

But now he was gone.

She saw it then, the overturned chair and the stain of coffee against the near wall, the shattered remains of a mug on the hardwood floor. "Oh, God," she murmured, barely able to breathe. She moved forward anyway, saw the brown envelope on the side of the table, the picture sitting on top. Of her. And Eric. Kissing passionately in the front of the deserted old diner, just a few doors down from the Blue Note, their bodies so intertwined they could have been making love.

And she knew. She knew why Eric had thrown his coffee against the wall and dumped over a chair. She knew why he didn't answer her call.

With shaking hands, Leigh grabbed a napkin, picked up the picture, turned it over.

A picture is worth a thousand words.
Maybe now you're ready to talk.

Leigh stepped into the hotel elevator and jabbed the button for the fifteenth floor, hoping against hope she wasn't too late. M. H. Cantrell had gone too far this time. The vile reporter who'd been hounding Eric for a story had left his hotel on the back of the photo. He thought that by threatening Eric he could secure the interview he sought.

He was wrong.

Eric wasn't about to talk to the media, especially the slimeball leading the charge linking him to genetic engineering. Eric Jones was too smart to risk having his words twisted into something that could be used against him in a court of law. He wasn't a man to be manipulated. He wasn't a man to be bullied.

Fool that he was, M. H. Cantrell had chosen to play his game with the wrong person.

The elevator stopped on the tenth floor, where two laughing teenage girls stepped inside and pressed the eleven button, forcing Leigh to bite down on the inside of her mouth.

"So help me God," Leigh heard the second she finally reached her destination. "If that picture shows up in one paper—*just one*—you will pay."

"I hardly think you're in a position to threaten me, Jones."

A hard, frustrated sound reverberated through the hotel corridor. "You have no idea what position I'm in, Cantrell. You have no idea what I'll do when backed into a corner. This is my life you're playing games with—"

Leigh saw Eric shove against the partially open door separating him from the wiry reporter and felt her heart flat out stop. "Eric, don't!"

He stopped abruptly, swung toward her. "This doesn't concern you, Leigh."

"He's not worth it," she said, hurrying toward them. "He can't hurt us."

Cantrell started to laugh. "Well, isn't this cozy? Lady Barracuda riding in to save the day."

Leigh saw Eric's body gather force and quickly inserted herself in the doorway between the two men. She turned to Eric, put her hands on his chest. "This isn't the answer."

His gaze hardened. "Neither is letting this slimebag ruin your reputation."

"A picture of me kissing you is hardly going to ruin my reputation," she said with a wry smile, then turned toward Cantrell. "But coercion and bribery may well ruin yours."

The smug man blanched. "Bribery?"

"You can hand over the negatives now," she said, slipping her hand in her purse and retrieving her mobile phone. "We can settle this just the three of us, or we can get the authorities involved. The choice is yours."

"I haven't committed a crime."

"Not yet," Leigh conceded. "But the second you run that picture, I'll have the cops on you so fast you won't have time to crawl back under your rock."

The little man lifted his chin, but defeat hollowed out his dark eyes. "I'm just trying to get a story."

"A story that doesn't exist," Eric said, moving to stand by her side. "A story based on lies and half truths."

"You're so damn cocksure," Cantrell spat, then slunk into his hotel room and retrieved a long white envelope from the desk. "But the truth will come out," he vowed, returning to the doorway. "It always does."

Eric took the envelope from Cantrell and removed the negatives, held them up toward the light. "How do we know these are the only copies you have?"

A little smile twisted the reporter's mouth. "You don't."

"Damn it, Cantrell—"

Leigh put her hand to Eric's forearm. "He's not going to run any pictures, Eric."

"But I am going to run the truth," the reporter snarled. "And the truth is that the government is keeping secrets from us all. There are at least five genetically engineered men and women living among us, walking time bombs ready to explode at any minute." Very pointedly, he met Leigh's gaze. "Don't say I didn't warn you."

Eric couldn't believe how badly he'd lost his cool. If Leigh hadn't shown up when she had, he could well be back behind bars, charged with assaulting a reporter. No way was he going to let that muckraker drag Leigh's name through the mud. If Eric fell, Leigh was not going with him.

Clenching his hands around his steering wheel, he stared at the snarl of downtown traffic, but saw only the glare of truth. Someone was playing him like a damn puppet, jerking his strings and watching him dance like a marionette in front of a firing squad, laughing as he twisted in the wind.

…at least five genetically engineered men and women living among us, walking time bombs ready to explode.

Cantrell's words echoed insidiously. The claim sounded insane, but Jake had confirmed truth to the reporter's words. Government files indicated genetic experimentation had occurred in the 1960s. Children had been born, manipulated, their memories erased. Allegedly these children had been sent to live with adoptive parents, where they'd grown to adulthood with no knowledge of their uniqueness.

With no knowledge of the danger they posed to everyone else.

Eric swore softly. Deep in his bones, he didn't believe he was one of those children, but he had no way to disprove Cantrell's theory. The Joneses had adopted him from an orphanage, where they'd received no information about his prior life. They knew only that a woman had surrendered him to the nuns, claiming she could no longer care for the energetic two-year-old.

Eric had never looked for her. The Joneses had been the only parents he needed.

But that didn't mean he hadn't wondered. What was his real mother like? His father? Whose dimple did he have? Whose blue eyes? Whose tall, athletic build? Whose throwing arm? Did he have any brothers or sisters? Nieces? Nephews?

As a child he'd felt guilty for those thoughts; as a man he felt angry. The answers didn't matter. His birth mother had decided that the night she surrendered him to the orphanage.

But now...now the answers could help prove he was a normal, average guy, not the product of genetic engineering.

But those answers, if they existed, had died with Susan Jones. Eric didn't even know the name of the orphanage from which he'd been adopted. Finding out had never seemed important.

Now the questions, the possibilities, gnawed. He fit the profile, damn it. He fit the profile.

Frowning, Eric turned onto Michigan Avenue. He and

Leigh had said their goodbyes at the hotel and gone their separate ways, agreeing to meet at her office toward the end of the day. His body burned at the memory of her sleeping in his big bed, seeing her long, dark hair fanned out on his white pillowcase, the way those strands had felt beneath his fingertips, like silk. He'd wanted to slide beside her and pull her against him, but—

The ringing of his mobile phone interrupted the dangerous thought. "Jones here."

"Eric, it's me."

The second he heard her voice, he knew something was wrong. "What's happened?" he asked, accelerating.

She sighed. "It's Hack."

A moment passed before the name clicked; Hack was the young man Leigh had contacted to look into the elaborate wire transfers and network of electronic trails. "Tell me."

"His apartment was torched," Leigh said. "Early this morning. He was inside asleep when it happened, but his cat woke him and they managed to escape through a window."

Eric swore softly. Regret slammed in, hard and fast. "They're watching us. They're watching every damn move."

"I know," Leigh said, and sounded tired. "But Hack is in a safe house now, and he managed to get his computer out with him."

Eric turned into the parking garage of Leigh's building. "Had he found anything?"

"He's not sure yet, but he did indicate he'd been following some interesting trails."

After taking a ticket, Eric headed up the ramp toward the Brightman and Associates visitor parking. Inside the bowels of the building, his mobile connection crackled.

"The signal's fading," he said. "I'll be there in a few minutes. We can talk more then."

"Okay." Leigh hesitated. "Eric...thanks."

He rounded the bend and looked for a spot. "Like I could stay away from you after last night."

The sound was distorted, but Leigh laughed. "...thoughtful of you," he made out. "...haven't opened...box...but I'm sure...beautiful."

Eric swung into a spot for a car much smaller than his. "What box?"

"...breaking up...see you...few minutes."

"Leigh, wait!" But it was too late. He looked at his mobile phone and saw the Call Ended signal.

Adrenaline spewed nastily. Eric turned off the car and threw open the door, not caring about the shiny black Mercedes in the way.

Then he ran.

He hadn't sent Leigh a box.

Leigh hung up the phone and leaned back in her chair, lifting a hand to rub the tension at her temples. Time was running out. The grand jury would convene in less than a week, and an indictment was looking more and more likely. They would go to trial then, and the nightmare would drag on.

She couldn't let that happen. She couldn't let Eric stand trial, go to prison for a crime he hadn't committed. She'd spoken with her private investigators earlier in the day, and they'd both been vague but optimistic about information they'd uncovered. Just a few more days, they'd promised. That was all they needed.

Hack had said the same. He'd indicated he didn't want to get her hopes up, but he'd accessed the World Bank system and found some strange echo trails. He'd found the same trails leading to her bank account, where sums of fifty thousand dollars appeared and vanished on a daily basis. He'd stumbled across something else, he'd said, but didn't go into detail.

Regret cut through her. Hack was a good kid, with an IQ she was sure registered off the charts. He should be attending the University of Chicago, not living in back alleys and hacking into computer systems for thrills. She'd been horrified to learn of the fire, that he'd lost everything but his computer, but he'd assured her he hadn't had much to lose.

Sadly, Leigh realized that was probably true.

She'd make it up to him, she vowed. They'd prove Eric's innocence and Hack would get the education he deserved.

Restless, she stood and crossed to the small conference table across her office, where the long narrow florist's box waited. Julia had brought it in just before Hack called. Leigh had gestured for her to place it on the table, but before she could open it, the phone had rung. She'd been so distracted by Hack's news she'd forgotten about Eric's gift, until she'd been on the phone with him and her gaze had snagged on the table.

Now she smiled, lifting the box and drawing it to her heart. She couldn't remember the last time someone had sent her flowers.

Very slowly, with great anticipation, she removed the thick red velvet ribbon from the box and lifted the lid, sifted through the crisp green tissue paper. Then her heart slammed into her ribs and everything inside her went horribly, deathly cold.

Eric strode from the elevator the second the doors slid open. "Julia, where's Leigh?"

The sharply dressed receptionist frowned. "In her office. Is something wrong?"

"Call security," he instructed, running down the hall. Several men and women stopped to stare, but he didn't care. He knew he looked like a crazy man. He felt like one, too.

At the door to Leigh's office, he didn't waste time knocking. He pushed inside, forgot to breathe.

She stood rigidly at the far side of the office, near the small conference table. "Leigh!"

She didn't move, just stood there staring at her feet, where decapitated black roses spilled from a long gold florist box.

Relief slammed in hard and fast, followed quickly by a blade of caution. And a surge of anger. He swore hotly and crossed to her, took her shoulders in his hands and turned her to face him. "Sweetheart?"

Her face was pale, her eyes dark and shocky. "I—I thought they were from you."

He knew better than to touch them, even though he doubted the flowers or box carried incriminating evidence. Instead, with his foot, he nudged the roses apart, revealing a small card, with a note scrawled in dark, menacing letters.

This is your last warning.

And something inside him shattered. Just shattered, breaking through ironclad constraints and seizing control.

"Goddamn it," he swore hotly, then took her cold hand in his and started for the door. "I'm done playing games."

* * *

Eric stood in a near-blinding slash of late-afternoon sun, staring out the sliding glass door of his apartment. Across the street three young boys sat on the steps of a redbrick brownstone, laughing and carrying on, but Leigh doubted Eric saw or heard. His back was rigid, his hands balled into tight fists, his feet shoulder-width apart. In one hand he held the glass of Scotch she'd given him so tightly she half expected him to crush the tumbler he'd yet to bring to his mouth. Even his clothes looked angry, the black of his pants appearing harsh and rigid, the gray of his knit shirt conveying the warning to stay away.

Leigh couldn't do that. Had never learned how, not when it came to this man. That had always, always been the problem.

He'd not said a word since he'd practically dragged her from her office. She'd protested, insisting they needed to call the authorities, but every unyielding line of his body indicated Eric Jones was done with authorities. Done with rules and regulations. Done being threatened and bullied. Done being played with.

The realization, the implications, alarmed more than the black roses and threatening note.

On the drive to his place there'd been a volatile glint to his eyes, but he'd not said a word as he took her hand and led her through the handful of reporters still loitering outside his brownstone. Now an unsettling energy radiated from his body, tightening around her chest to the point she could barely breathe. She'd never seen him like this, coldly furious and just barely hanging on, like a steam piston ready to blow.

And she couldn't stand it. Couldn't stand the excruciating quiet, couldn't stand the absolute stillness, couldn't stand not knowing.

"Eric," she said, crossing to him. "Tell me what you're thinking."

His body went even more rigid. "You don't want to hear what I'm thinking right now."

The words were harsh, coarse, clearly meant to warn her away. But Leigh kept right on going. "Then why did you bring me here?"

"You really have to ask me that?" he bit out.

The urge to step closer, to lay a hand against the hard planes of his back was strong, but instinct cautioned she take this slowly.

You have no idea what I'll do when backed into a corner.

No, she didn't. That was what worried her.

"Eric, please," she said, calling upon the voice she'd found effective in eliciting testimony from reluctant witnesses. "You've never been a man to shut down like this. Don't start now."

"How do you know that, Leigh?" he asked in an ominously quiet voice. "How do you know what kind of man I am? A lot happens in ten years."

She sucked in a sharp breath, let it out slowly. "Lives change," she conceded, "but people rarely do."

He spun toward her in a near-violent rush of movement, revealing eyes glittering with an intensity that sent her heart stammering into a crazy staccato rhythm.

"Damn it, Leigh," he ground out, "leave it alone, okay?" The lines of his face were harsh, his jaw darkened by whiskers he'd not taken time to shave that morning. "I'm trying to do what's best for you here. I'm trying to do the right thing." He stepped toward her and lifted a hand, but abruptly aborted the movement.

"Don't you understand?" he asked, and the question

sounded pained. "I don't trust myself with you right now, and you shouldn't either."

She struggled to breathe, to think. "Don't be ridiculous," she said as levelly as she could. "I know you're not some genetically engineered quirk of nature. You didn't commit the World Bank heist and you're not pre-programmed to hurt me."

"But I might do this." Before she realized his intent, he closed the distance between them and took her face in his hands, put his mouth to hers and drank deep. The kiss was hard and sudden, strong and thoroughly possessive. His lips moved against hers restlessly, as though he'd been waiting a lifetime to taste her, absorb her, and might never have the chance again.

"Ten years," he rasped, pulling back and sliding his hands into her hair. "Ten years I've wanted to touch you again, taste you, discover if what we shared that night was as amazing as I remember, and now here you are again."

"Eric—"

"Do you have any idea what this is doing to me, Leigh?" The question sounded ripped from somewhere deep inside him, somewhere dark and anguished. "To know you're finally back in my life, after all these years, to see your smile and hear your voice?" He urged her closer, making it impossible not to feel the rigid planes of his body. Not to know how badly he wanted. "To know that you're here and you're real, only to face the possibility of losing you again? Of you being hurt—*again*—because of me?"

The ragged stream of words staggered her. Just staggered. She was a highly educated, highly experienced attorney. She made a living out of gathering evidence and making compelling arguments, but as she stared at

Eric, felt his hands playing with her hair and his body pressed to hers, she could no more string words together than she could pull away. "Eric—"

Something wild and primal flashed in his eyes. "It tears me up, Leigh. It makes me wish I'd never walked into your office."

Her heart clenched. "But you did," she whispered. And in doing so, he'd set their lives on a collision course beyond his wildest imagination.

He untangled a hand from her hair and slid it to the side of her face, where he extended his thumb toward her mouth. "Yes, I did. Selfish bastard that I am, I never once stopped to think about the impact on you, and now your life is on the line."

Wherever he skimmed, she burned. Tingles streaked through her like wildfire. "We don't know that," she pointed out, trying to focus and not feel. "All we know is we're getting close and someone is running scared."

He swore softly. "Those threats are real," he countered relentlessly with both words and caresses. "And they're dangerous. Whoever is playing fast and loose with my life means business, and I'd rather go to prison than let you get taken down in the crossfire."

The harsh words penetrated the haze of sensation, making her wince and reminding her how high the stakes had climbed. "That's not going to happen."

But once set on a course of action, Eric Jones had never been a man to turn away. "I've tried, damn it," he said, sliding a palm along her back and pressing her to his body. "I've tried to play by your rules."

The frustration in his voice pulsed through her, ramming up against defenses that longed to crumble. "It's not about rules," she denied, but her voice broke on the words, betraying all that she could not allow herself to say. It was about right and wrong, smart and rash, caution and foresight. It was about one bitterly cold night and choices etched in betrayal that could not be taken back, decisions that had the power to shatter the lives of a man who'd already endured too much and an innocent little boy who'd yet to learn how cruel fate could be.

Eric's gaze darkened. "Every time I see you, all those years vanish and it's all I can do not to touch you like this." He skimmed his palm up her side to slide over an aching breast. "To kiss you," he added as his mouth slid along hers, open this time, gentle but demanding.

Everything inside her was melting, melting, puddling into a need and desire that practically blinded her. She wanted this. She wanted this man's hands on her body. His mouth on hers. She wanted to be underneath him, to have him inside her. She wanted to hold on tight and never let go. She'd wanted that for ten long years, had awakened bathed in sweat and burning from the memory of his touch more times than she cared to remember.

But the truth remained hovering just out of reach, warning Leigh to turn back now. While she still could.

Before it was too late.

"Eric—"

"I lost you once, Leigh. I'm not going to let that happen again."

"You might not have a choice," she whispered, and felt moisture well in her eyes.

Eric pulled back enough so that his gaze met hers. "We all have choices," he murmured, wiping away the tears she couldn't stop. "We can choose to live in fear of tomorrow or we can grab hold of the here and now, make the most of every moment we do have."

The quiet words destroyed her.

"I'm not going to hurt you," he whispered, returning

his mouth to hers. "So help me God, I promise I'll never hurt you again."

Leigh's heart clenched with the truth. She heard the passion in Eric's voice, the intensity, but she knew his promise was one that could not be kept. Every instinct for self-preservation, every molecule of caution, every grain of sanity, demanded she turn and walk away. *Now*.

But fascination held her motionless.

Eric Jones the lanky, cocksure grad student, she'd known inside and out. But Eric Jones the hardened confident man, she did not, and he intrigued her as no man ever had. Like a prism, every moment they spent together revealed new facets to his personality—his strength and loyalty, his determination, his fierce protectiveness, his gentle but demanding passion—and each of them thrilled her in ways she inherently recognized as dangerous.

Too bad she'd never been a woman to shy away from danger.

This man had the power to destroy her in ways from which she would never recover. But she, too, had the power to forever change his life. Doing so would cost her greatly, cost her everything, but she had no choice.

"What if I hurt you?" she asked quietly.

"That's a chance I'm willing to take," he said against her mouth, urging her to open to him, share with him.

She did. The heat of desire licked through her body, sending her melting into him, just like that night so long ago. She tried valiantly to remind herself of all the reasons making love with Eric was wrong, would only lead to heartbreak, but the more deeply he kissed her, the more possessively his mouth took hers, the more relentlessly his hands skimmed her body, the more all rational thought abandoned her, replaced by a blinding desire she'd thought long destroyed. The need had survived, strengthened as it lay dormant, simmering and waiting for the day Eric Jones walked back into her life, touched her as though he could never get enough, kissed her as though she was the only woman in the world.

Deep, deep inside, something slipped and gave way. Logic? Caution? Self-preservation? Leigh didn't know, and in that moment, didn't care. She only knew that the man she'd never stopped loving, never stopped wanting, had stepped out of her dreams and once again filled her with a soul-piercing longing.

Only Eric had ever made her feel this way.

Last night she'd drifted to sleep to the slow, steady rhythm of his heart. She heard that rhythm again, but now it was neither slow nor steady. It thrummed hard and erratic, like hers.

"Tell me no," he whispered, working at the small buttons of her silk blouse. "Tell me to stop, and I will."

Ten

Stop.

The word lodged in her throat, trapped behind a surge of emotion. In some shrinking corner of her mind, Leigh knew she should do as he challenged. Tell him no. Tell him to stop. Because he would. He wasn't a man to force her, no matter how badly the rigid planes of his body revealed he wanted her.

But rather than pull from him, Leigh slid a hand along his back and pressed him closer, reveled in the feel of hard muscles bunched in control. The bone-deep passion, the soul-shattering love, had been repressed for too many years. Now that his mouth moved against hers, that his fingers slipped inside her bra and teased her nipple, she could no more deny the need to have him inside her than she could deny the need to breathe.

All those walls she'd erected against him, the barriers she'd nurtured and defenses she'd fortified, they dissolved like mist, leaving only a crystalline need that had burned hot for ten years. Sensation obliterated reason, desire overran caution.

One moment. One night. One memory.

"No," she whispered. "No."

Eric went very still, his hand against her breast, his body against hers. His breathing was hard and labored, but when he pulled back, she saw only a hot glow to his eyes.

And she smiled. She wanted this man, had always wanted his man. Loved this man. Had always loved this man.

"No, don't stop," she clarified. "Don't ever, ever stop."

He hadn't. In the years that stood between them, Eric had never stopped thinking of her, remembering, wanting. Even when an ocean separated them, when he'd pledged his life to another, when he'd learned she might be doing the same. He'd never gotten Leigh out of his system, out of his blood. He'd never stopped wondering. Never stopped hungering. At times, driven by a cutting need to quit punishing himself, he'd told himself that memory had embellished the draw between them, the passion and intensity, that the sorry state of his marriage had caused him to seek solace in the past.

Now he knew the truth.

Nothing had been embellished. Not one detail, one nuance. If anything, memory had numbed the edges of the desire. Otherwise he doubted he could have lived ten years without her, not if every morning he'd felt this incredible rush, only to be denied the ability to touch and taste, to see, to make her his.

But she was here now, and she wanted him as badly as he wanted her. He drank in the sight of her standing in a wash of late-afternoon sun, from her silky long hair to her heavy-lidded brown eyes, the glow to her skin and her slightly parted mouth.

"Make love to me, Eric," she whispered in that husky voice of hers, the one that sounded not at all like an attorney, but everything like a lover. "Please."

The please got him. He'd wanted to draw the moment out, to stretch every kiss, every caress to the breaking point, but when she looked at him through those slumberous eyes, he was lost. In a heartbeat he had her in his arms and down the hall, to his room where his big bed waited, the bed she'd slept in the night before, the bed by which he'd stood, silently standing guard.

And wanting.

There'd be no sleeping this night, no standing guard. At least not yet.

But there was plenty of wanting. It seared through him, blurring his vision. He wanted to taste and touch every inch of her, to prove he would never hurt her again. To make this good for her, to make up for the way it had been all those years before, when he'd taken her virginity then walked away. To show her she had nothing to fear from him, that this time he'd play it by the heart, not a misplaced sense of right and wrong, duty and responsibility. His need for this woman ran deeper than the physical. Always had. Living without her had been like living without a fundamental part of himself.

"I never stopped wanting you," he told her, sliding her down the length of his body to her feet. "Never stopped remembering."

"Neither did I." A slow smile curved her face as she lifted her hands to his chest and let them slide lower, to the waistband of his black pants. There she dipped inside and put her cool palms to his abdomen. "I'd see you in my dreams," she whispered, moving up and sliding the cotton knit shirt over his shoulders. "I'd see that look in your eyes and I'd know you wanted me as badly as I wanted you."

A moan ripped from his throat.

"I saw you, too," he said, fighting the tiny buttons of her silk shirt. Impatience ripped at him, but he forced himself to go slow, as he'd promised. He'd waited ten years. He could wait ten minutes. "You would smile," he said, "like you're doing now."

The curve of her mouth widened as she lifted her face to his chest and pressed her mouth to his wide, flat nipple.

Pleasure shivered through him. "Not fair," Eric practically growled. He wanted to do as she did, to put his mouth to her breast and taste, to tease in an erotically slow rhythm, to drive her mad with need.

Leigh let out a throaty laugh, joining her hands to his and quickly finishing the job on the buttons. He slid the silky fabric from her shoulders, then stepped back to admire the sight of her standing in his bedroom, wearing nothing but a pair of cream linen trousers and a lacy taupe bra. Her breasts swelled from the scalloped edges, making him burn even hotter.

"In my dreams," she whispered, smiling with a hint of vulnerability so uncharacteristic that it sliced to the bone, "you'd tease me until I cried out."

He almost lost it right then and there. Somewhere along the line the girl had become a woman, and the woman promised to be his undoing. "Lucky me," he murmured, flicking free the front clasp. Her breasts were fuller than before, her nipples larger and darker. "Like this?" he asked, sliding his tongue around the aureole.

She lifted a hand to hold his head in place. "Just like that."

A hard sound of primal male hunger ripped from inside him as he felt her fingers dig deeper. He wanted to keep teasing her, teasing himself, but the need to have her fully in his mouth was too great. He sucked the peak in and worked it with his mouth, while she writhed, soft sounds of satisfaction echoing through the room.

"Eric," she whispered, backing him toward the bed. "Please."

He needed no more encouragement than that. They quickly discarded their pants and found the mattress, she stretching out languidly, he easing alongside her. All the while he kissed and caressed, his mouth exploring hers, sliding along her neck, again finding her breasts, then her abdomen, next the scrap of lacy taupe panties clinging to her slender hips. He eased the panties down with his hands and slid his mouth lower, lower, until the heat surrounded him and her body tensed. He tasted her, felt her shiver.

"With you," she said breathlessly, her hands sliding along his slick back and urging him back up. "Please...not alone."

The wave of tenderness blindsided him, prompting him to slide up her body and return his mouth to hers. Her arms and legs immediately closed around him, holding him to her as though she never wanted to let go.

"Not alone," he assured, moving his mouth against hers. He refused to think of how many nights they'd spent alone, with only dreams to sustain them. "Never again." Determination hammered through him, to prove she had no reason to fear tomorrow, that this time would be different. This time he'd be there when she needed him.

The thought of prison nudged the haze of desire, but he forced it aside. He was not going to prison, damn it. He was not going to lose Leigh. The past couldn't hurt them, and, he vowed as he slipped a hand between her legs and found her slick and ready, neither could the future.

"Please," she whispered, arching her hips into his hand. "Now."

He needed no more invitation than that. He shifted slightly and slid inside, found her small and tight, much as she had been that night a lifetime ago. She tilted her hips and welcomed him deep, welcomed him home. He wanted to savor the sensation, but found himself pulling out, only to sink back in. Again and again. More deliberately each time. He loved the way her eyes glazed over and her head lolled to the side, the way she matched him stroke for stroke, urged him deep. They found a steady rhythm, rocking, rocking, slick bodies sliding together, faster each time.

"Yes," she whispered, fingernails digging into his back. "Oh, yes."

And when she arched up and cried out his name, he didn't try to hold on for one second longer. He let himself go, thrusting deeper into the heat that had haunted him for ten long years. In some hazy corner of his mind he heard his primal sound of release, heard her match it with one of her own. Then there was only sensation, the feel of her grasping him, crying out his name, of losing himself, finally, at last, in Leigh.

Only Leigh.

They came together again in the still of the night, made love during those quiet, fragile minutes before dawn broke on the horizon and ushered in a new day. Joy and despair curled through her, slipping into her chest and squeezing her heart. While one rejoiced, the other reminded. Tears stung her eyes even as Eric moved inside her. This was what she'd wanted. For too many years she'd woken abruptly from dreams so real and intense her body had burned from the remembered promise of Eric's touch.

She'd told herself she was being foolish. She'd told

herself she'd romanticized and glorified what she and Eric had shared. That she'd let memory spin itself into something far more fantastic than reality could ever offer.

She'd been wrong.

They moved together now, and with every powerful thrust of his hips, she felt a little more of herself slip and give way. She loved this man. She loved him wholly and irrevocably, against logic and caution and better judgment. She'd given him her heart years before, and despite secrets and hurts that lurked between them, she'd never gotten that fundamental piece of herself back.

And now she knew she never would.

The sun was already starting to filter through the wooden blinds slanting across the window, and just as they had on that bitterly cold morning so long ago, soon they'd say goodbye.

This time, forever.

Eric Jones stood accused, but she was the one who'd committed the wrong. She was the one who'd been judge and jury, who'd rendered a fate without granting him so much as a by-your-leave. And no matter how noble her intentions had been, no matter how deeply she loved him, the truth cut harder and deeper with every caress of his lips. His body. She'd robbed this man of something precious and fundamental. There was no way to change the truth, no magic door through time and space to undo mistakes and regrets.

There was only the here and now, and the unstoppable certainty of what lay ahead.

"Leigh," he murmured, threading his fingers through hers and moving more powerfully within her. "I'll never let you go."

They came together like that, hand to hand, body to

body, heart to heart, while deep inside, Leigh slowly, quietly, shattered. One moment, one decision, one mistake.

No dream lasted forever.

She awoke slowly, gently, to the rumble of thunder in the distance. She shifted in the tangled sheets, felt the rush of cool air against the exposed flesh of her shoulder. Awareness nudged at her, but she blocked it, not ready to let go of the erotic dream that had her blood humming. *Eric.* He'd been gentle, thorough. He'd touched her in ways she'd never been touched, brought her body singing to life with a ferocity she hadn't known possible.

Contentment hummed deep.

Lightning flickered against the darkness of semi-sleep, another low roar of thunder. She felt herself start to drift through the warm, thick layers of sensation that had buffeted her during the night. There was heat and desire, a wave of fulfillment that tightened her chest.

Then the bed shifted.

The haze crumbled, scraping away sensation and revealing the reality that she wasn't alone. She hadn't been dreaming. She and Eric had spent the night in bed, claiming each other's bodies with an urgency that staggered. They'd slept little during the long, hot hours while evening had slipped into night, trying to sate years worth of wanting in mere hours.

"Sleep, sweetheart," he murmured in a roughened voice as his mouth came down against hers. The kiss was soft, achingly tender.

Leigh held her breath, but could do nothing about the rapid pounding of her heart. She didn't open her eyes, didn't want him to know she was awake. Wasn't ready to face him.

Thunder boomed nearby, rattling the bedroom windows. And then Eric was gone. She heard his footsteps moving against the hardwood floor, and only then did she allow herself to face the morning. Throat tight, she watched him walk naked from the bedroom and into the bathroom. He didn't bother closing the door, just reached into the bathtub and turned on the shower. A moment later he stepped inside and yanked the white curtain closed.

Everything came surging back, every delicious, hot moment. Every mistake. Emotion broke from her heart and rushed her eyes, and for the first time in years, she didn't bother fighting the sorrow. She wanted to follow Eric into the bathroom, to step into the shower with him, to feel his warm hands slide a bar of soap over her breasts and stomach. To do the same to him. With her mouth and her fingers she'd explored every hard contour of his body the night before, and deep inside, she burned to do the same by daylight, to taste and treasure.

To feel him taste and treasure her.

The ache sharpened, deepened, not tightening around her chest, but lancing through it.

She knew what she had to do. She'd stolen her moment, made her mistake. Now she had no choice.

Quietly, Leigh slipped from bed and found her bra and panties on the floor where Eric had discarded them. She gathered her slacks and blouse, could barely make her shaking hands fight with the buttons. The seconds ticked by excruciatingly fast. She grabbed her shoes and headed for the door, not allowing herself a glance back at the bathroom, where water still rattled through old pipes.

She'd already made her choice, she reminded as she

stepped into the rain, looking for a taxi and thanking God no reporters remained.

Leaving Eric was the hardest thing she'd ever done, but deep inside, she knew the pain was nothing compared to what lay ahead.

There was no turning back. Hadn't been for a long time.

He wanted to be angry with her. He wanted to be furious. While he'd been standing under the spray of lukewarm water, imagining her there with him, the feel of her flesh as he slid a bar of soap along her curves, she'd rolled from his bed and dressed, turned and walked away.

Just as he'd done that morning so long ago.

The truth scraped hard. One night, no matter how raw and explosive, could not tear down the monolith that stood between them.

Eric swung his car off the boulevard and onto a side street shaded by ancient elms and maples. The yellow glow of the sinking sun barely seeped through the thick, heavily leafed canopies. Sprawling brick houses lined both sides of the street, an occasional car or SUV parked out front.

So this was where she lived, Eric thought as he cruised past a young woman in Lycra jogging down the sidewalk. He took in the scatter of basketball goals and skateboards, scooters and bicycles, and felt his frustration slip a notch.

He'd wanted to go after her the second he'd found her gone. He'd wanted to follow, to force her to confront all that had passed between them, not just in the past, but the night before. She'd come apart in his arms, had welcomed him into her body with the same urgency ripping through him.

Regret twisted with understanding. More than just years separated them, and he knew it. A lifelong prison sentence loomed on his horizon. One night of mind-blowing sex couldn't clear his name, couldn't grant them a future. He deserved her caution. He'd hurt her badly once before.

This time would be different, he vowed as he matched the address he'd jotted down with the numbers on the two-story red-brick house with a welcoming front porch. He swung into the driveway, stopping abruptly to avoid running over the mud-caked dirt bike lying on its side. This time he would do everything he'd not done before. He would stay. He would not let a misplaced sense of duty lead him astray. He would do whatever it took to be the man Leigh needed him to be.

He would not go down, would not let go, not without a fight.

This is your last warning.

Eric turned off the engine, but could do nothing to stop the memory from grinding through him. She was right. They *were* getting close, making someone nervous. But whereas she saw that as a positive sign, he saw only the danger. To her.

And that was something he could not allow.

He stepped into the muggy air of early evening. The day had crawled by, but he'd been determined to give Leigh the space she obviously needed. One truth remained clear, a truth he would not let her run from. Last night had only been the beginning. The clock no longer ticked against them. They had the days and weeks ahead, and every moment that lay beyond.

Eric glanced at the house, not surprised to see clay pots overflowing with geraniums and petunias artfully arranged on the porch. The boxwood hedges were neatly trimmed, lined in front by waving fountain grass and cheerful clusters of pink impatiens. From the back, he heard barking, and wondered if the dog belonged to Leigh. So much he didn't know about her, her life.

The basketball goal caught him by surprise.

The rusty post stretched high against the pale-blue sky, but the net looked brand new. Odd, Eric thought, then remembered the way a twenty-year-old Leigh had sweet-talked her way into more than one pick-up game. She'd held her own, too, maybe even used her femininity to steal the ball and sink a shot.

Eric followed a curved cement path to the front door, fighting the wave of nostalgia that crowded closer with every step. Impossible to walk this path and not think of all that had never been. All he'd once wanted. This was the life he'd seen for himself, a quiet neighborhood of tidy lawns and graceful trees, where neighbors helped out in a pinch and children played safely in front yards.

He and Becky had managed the house, but that was all.

The children had never come. Once, Eric had imagined himself a father, teaching a daughter with her mother's silky black hair and intelligent eyes how to ride a bicycle. He'd seen himself playing ball with sons who'd inherited his sandy-brown hair and killer throwing arm, who shared his love of baseball.

And his blood.

The swift blade of regret caught Eric by surprise. He'd long since adjusted to the fact he knew no one who shared his genetics. It didn't matter why his birth parents hadn't kept him. The Joneses had been wonderful people, he reminded himself as he knocked against the wooden door. They'd given him the best childhood imaginable. They'd loved him, made him their son in every way that mattered.

...*five genetically engineered men and women living among us, walking time bombs ready to explode at any minute.*

The memory of Cantrell's words sliced deep, bringing a fresh surge of anger. The reporter didn't know what the hell he was talking about. Eric would—

The front door swung open, and every vow he'd been about to make shattered.

"Hi, there," a young boy greeted. The kid looked to be somewhere around nine or ten, with thick brown hair and piercing blue eyes. He wore a baseball uniform, with grass stains at the knees. "Can I help you?"

Eric just stared. "I'm sorry," he forced himself to say. "I must have the wrong house. I was looking for Leigh Montgomery."

The boy flashed a crooked little smile, revealing a dimple that almost stopped Eric's heart cold. "You're in the right place," he said, then called over his shoulder. "Mom! Some guy's here to see you!"

Mom.

The word slammed into Eric, sending his heart jackhammering against his ribs.

Mom.

Sweet Christ. This boy was Leigh's son.

"Who is it?" she called, then emerged from what looked to be a family room with a dishtowel draped over her arm. Then she stopped abruptly. Instead of the professional, tailored suits she favored at the office, she wore a Cubs tank top and ratty, cutoff denim shorts that revealed her incredible long legs, the ones she'd wrapped around him the night before. She had her long, dark hair pulled into a ponytail.

The second he saw her eyes, wide with shock and drenched with horror, he knew. God almighty, he knew, and he flat-out quit breathing.

"It's me," he said in a hoarse voice he barely recognized.

"Eric."

Recognition ambushed him, sharp and fast and brutal. The boy's eyes. Good God, he knew those eyes...saw them in the mirror every morning. He had pictures in a box back at his apartment, pictures from another lifetime, another family. Looking at the boy was like tumbling back in time and landing in territory that was both achingly familiar and horrifyingly foreign.

He needed no confirmation, not when the evidence stared at him. Leigh had given birth to a child—*his child.*

He had a son.

"Connor," Leigh said in a voice he could tell she fought to steady. "Why don't you take Bruiser for a walk before it gets dark?"

The boy glanced at Eric, then back at his mom. "Are you...sure? I mean, I can stay if you like."

Eric's chest tightened. Protecting her. The boy—*his son*—was protecting her. From Eric.

His father.

The blast of anger prompted him to curl his hands into tight fists. Incredulity choked him.

"I'm sure," Leigh said, crossing the braided rug in the foyer to ruffle her son's shaggy brown hair. "Everything's fine."

The boy, Connor she'd called him, didn't look convinced, but he shrugged anyway and headed to the back of the house, glancing at them once before vanishing around a corner.

And then Eric and Leigh were left standing in the open doorway, alone with the lie, and the truth.

Hard realities tore through Eric, badgering relentlessly at a control he felt slipping. The truth drilled deep. He waited, though, waited until he heard the back door slam shut before he trusted himself to speak.

"That's my child," he ground out. "My son."

Typical fearless Leigh, she lifted her chin and didn't back down. "He has your eyes," she said in a voice suddenly strong and sure. "And your throwing arm."

"Sweet Jesus." Shock clouded his vision. "How could you?" he asked raggedly. Just the night before she'd given him her body, but she'd kept the truth—a fundamental truth—locked away from him. All those years. All those long, empty years when his mother had withered away, longing for a grandchild, she'd had one. She'd had a grandson who looked exactly like Eric at that age.

"We made love last night, for God's sake. How could you be with me like that, but neglect to mention that we'd created a child?"

He saw her swallow hard. "I was going to tell you after the case."

Something inside him broke and gave way. "After the case? Isn't that about ten years too late?"

She closed her eyes, opened them to a pain so bottomless it ripped at the hard edges of his anger. "I can't change the past."

Questions hammered through him. The need to know why, to understand almost sent him to his knees. So much made sense now, horrible sense. Her hesitancy, the dread he'd occasionally caught in her gaze. He wanted to charge into her cozy little house, where he could feel the cool blast of the air conditioning. But he didn't trust himself to be alone with her now. Didn't trust the sharp emotions slicing him up inside.

"Does he know?" Eric asked.

Her mouth tightened. "No."

"Does he think I'm dead?"

Moisture rushed to her eyes. "No."

"Does he think I didn't want him?" The thought sickened.

"No," Leigh said with a desperation he'd never heard from her. "I'd never do that."

He looked at her standing there in the inviting foyer of her house, the woman who'd been naked in his bed the night before, who'd cried out his name and dug her fingernails into his back, but saw only a stranger. A fragment of a coed he'd once known, the shadow of a woman he'd thought he loved.

Disbelief collided with the hot sting of betrayal.

"I don't know what you'd do anymore," he said roughly. "The Leigh I knew would never have lied about something like this."

"But the Eric I knew did go home to marry someone else," she reminded quietly. "He did love another."

That stopped him cold. He heard the pain in her voice, saw it in her defiant brown eyes, and realized she spoke the truth.

Or at least he'd thought it was the truth at the time.

He stepped into the shadowy foyer and lifted his hands to her face, wiped at the warm, quiet tears spilling over her lashes. He'd only seen her cry once before, the night his father had died, when the two of them had cried together.

And created a child.

"I loved you, too," he told her raggedly.

She twisted away in a near-violent rush of movement, as though his touch hurt as badly as his actions had. "Don't!" Fury flashed in her eyes. "Don't touch me, and so help me God, don't tell me you loved me."

The control he'd been fighting to hold on to snapped. "Damn it, Leigh, what do you want me to do?" he demanded, lifting his hands to her shoulders. "I suddenly find out that I've got a nine-year-old son I knew nothing about, and you expect me to just take the news in stride? Would you rather I say that you never meant anything to me? That we just had raw sex that night and I never thought of you again? Never imagined what it would have been like if I hadn't had to go home and bury my father, help my mother? If I hadn't already been in so deep with Becky that I worried that if I left her she'd lose her will to live, in addition to use of her legs? Is that what you want to hear? That you were just a casual one-night stand and that I don't give a damn that we made a child together? That *this* doesn't change *everything?*"

Leigh angled her chin. "If that's the truth, yes."

He swore hotly, but before he could say anything, an angry voice resounded from behind Leigh.

"Mom? Is it true? Is this man my father?"

Eleven

Leigh went horribly still. Every coherent thought, every jagged emotion, crashed into a dizzying rush of dread. She felt herself sway, felt Eric's hands on her arms tighten in a mockery of support.

"Let go," she mouthed to him, and despite the thinning line of his lips, he did. Very slowly, very deliberately, she turned from his piercing blue eyes toward her son, who stood behind her in the shadowy foyer with the dog leash in his hand and questions in his blue, blue eyes.

"Mom?" He stepped closer. "You okay?"

She felt Eric step behind her, found herself ridiculously grateful for the moment of solidarity. "I'm fine," she said through the tightness in her throat. "I thought you were walking Bruiser."

His gaze narrowed. "I heard raised voices."

She forced a smile. That was her son, ever the protector. "Everything's fine."

Connor looked beyond her to Eric, who stood so close she could feel his chest rising and falling against her back. "Is it true? Is this guy my dad?"

Leigh felt herself sway, felt Eric slide a hand to her waist. Gratitude welled dizzily. She'd seen the cold fury in his eyes, felt it in his touch, but here in front of their son, he was showing only support.

The reality of that shredded her control in ways she didn't understand.

All these years. All these years she'd been as honest with her son as she could, telling him his father couldn't be with them, but that he would if he could. But now Eric was here, and her son deserved the truth.

But God help her, she'd always thought she'd have time to prepare. That she'd know just the right thing to say. That the words, the truth, would be gentle.

She'd never imagined standing between the two of them, between father and son who shared more than just genetics and blood, who shared eyes and a throwing arm, a love of baseball and the crisp fall air, with both of them watching her through laser-blue eyes, demanding that she confirm their relationship.

"Connor," she said, reaching out to ruffle his sandy hair badly in need of a cut. "This is Eric Jones, an old friend of mine from college."

A sheen of excitement replaced the apprehension in Connor's gaze. "The bank robber?"

Behind her, Eric tensed, his hand tightening against her side. "He didn't do it."

Connor's cheeks were flushed, his eyes dancing with awe. "Wow! And he's my dad?"

Leigh stared at her son, searching for the right words. But in the end, there was only one. "Yes."

Connor did nothing for a moment, just stared at Leigh and Eric. Then slowly, a smile broke on his face, so wide and deep, his dimple winked devilishly. "Cool," he breathed. "Wait till I tell my friends!"

Leigh reached for him. "Connor—"

"Are you going to move in with us?" he asked, slipping past her to stare up at his father.

"No," Leigh answered before Eric could. The word

left her throat raw. Any chance the three of them had possessed of being a real family had swirled away the moment she'd decided to keep the truth from Eric. "Mr. Jones lives downtown."

Connor's expression crumpled, his gaze never leaving Eric's. "But don't you want to be with us?"

The disappointment in his voice slashed deep.

Eric went down on one knee, all the tension and anger that had hardened his face moments before replaced by a warm smile. "More than you can imagine," he answered in the strong, assuring voice that had first melted Leigh's heart over a decade before.

"Then why?" Connor asked, suddenly sounding nothing at all like the little man he usually aspired to be, but everything like a nine-year-old kid who'd grown up without his dad.

Leigh shot Eric a sharp glance. "It's complicated," she hedged. "We can talk more after Mr. Jones is gone."

"But he just got here," Connor said, his mouth trembling.

Eric and Leigh exchanged another look. "I'll be back," he promised, pushing up to his full height. His hand found Connor's shoulder, as though he couldn't bring himself to quit touching the boy.

Connor stared up at his father, the full-grown replica of the man he was destined to become. "You're not…going to prison, are you?"

Agony shot through Eric's gaze, but only conviction sounded in his voice. "No, I'm not going to prison." Then he smiled. "Don't you have more confidence in your mom than that?"

The boy cast a sheepish look toward Leigh. "Well, yeah."

She forced a laugh, though deep inside she bled. "You'd better," she said with a levity she didn't come close to feeling.

He grinned at her, then back toward Eric. "You like baseball?"

Eric smiled. "Very much."

"I play shortstop. Hope to play for the Cubs one day. My team won our first playoff game today and I've got another game tomorrow. Wanna come?"

No, Leigh thought maniacally. No. But before she could voice the words, Eric spoke. "I'd like that," he said quietly. "I played shortstop, too."

Connor's eyes were dancing now, excitement shining bright. "Really? I think A-Rod is the greatest. I'm not that good yet, but someday..."

"I bet you will."

Leigh's chest tightened as she watched the two of them, stunned but not at all surprised by the easy rapport they fell into. Years separated father and son, but blood bound them. If ever a man had been born to be a father, that man was Eric. He would never forgive her deception, nor would he take it out on his son. He would accept him and love him, and in doing so he would be the father Connor had always dreamed of, the kind who attended baseball games and helped with homework, who listened and guided, who taught. And most of all, who loved.

Emotion jammed her throat, moisture filling her eyes. Outside the sun sank lower, stealing the last vestiges of light.

"Con," she said, "your father and I have a lot to talk about."

The boy looked from Eric to her, his expression one of acceptance. "Yeah, yeah," he grumbled. "I know.

Take Bruiser for a walk.'' Then he swung back toward
Eric. "I'm glad you're here. Mom always said you were
a good guy, but I didn't know if I'd ever get the chance
to meet you.''

Briefly, Eric's gaze met Leigh's, but just as quickly,
he returned his attention to his son and squeezed his
shoulder. "I'll be at your game tomorrow.''

"Awesome!'' Connor said, then scampered out with
the dog, once again leaving Eric and Leigh alone.

Moments dragged by with unbearable precision, each
carving out the ache in her chest. She knew she should
say something, but words wouldn't form. Just looking
at Eric, the pain in his eyes, shattered.

"I want my son, Leigh.'' The words were hard, his
eyes dark and demanding. "I'm not going to miss out
on any more of his life.''

"I would never ask you to.''

He glanced out the still-open front door, to where
Connor and his golden retriever, Bruiser, skidded down
the driveway. "We'll get married,'' he said, turning
back to her. There was no emotion in his voice, no
warmth, just cold, brittle fact. "Just as soon as it can be
arranged. We'll—''

"No.'' She stopped him, dizzy and disoriented and
devastated. Leigh wasn't sure how she stayed standing.
How many years she'd dreamed of Eric asking her to
marry him, of the warmth that would be in his voice,
the love in his eyes. The dreams they would share, the
future they would build. "No.''

He closed the distance between them and took her
upper arms in his hands. "The boy deserves a family.''

"He has a family,'' she shot back. "He has me and
my mother, and now he has you.''

"I won't be a part-time father.''

"And I don't want you to be," she insisted. "But marriage isn't the answer. We don't even know each other anymore."

He made a sound low in his throat. "We knew each other pretty damn well last night."

The memory flashed through her, but rather than heating, it chilled. This, she thought brokenly…this was what she'd tried to avoid all those years ago. "It takes more than sex to make a marriage work."

His gaze bore down on her. "We share a child, Leigh."

"And that child deserves a real family," she shot back, ten years worth of pent-up emotion and heartbreak spilling free. "He deserves parents who love each other as much as they love him, not two people who are stuck with each other by some arcane sense of responsibility."

"Goddamn it—"

"Eric—"

"This isn't about honor, Leigh. It's about a child. *My* child." He swore softly, the cold mask of fury slipping to reveal a sliver of pain that sliced to the bone. "How could you keep this from me, Leigh? How could you keep my son from me?"

The question was soft and ragged, and it completely ripped her to shreds. From the day she'd discovered she was carrying Eric's child, part of her had dreamed about telling him. Over the years, she'd found herself watching friends who became pregnant, the way their husbands doted on them, took care of them, smiled at them. There was always a light glowing in their eyes, a sheer joy, and she'd sometimes found her heart twisting at the thought of Eric looking at her like that, at him keeping a hand at the small of her back, watching every move she made. She'd sometimes imagined that light in his eyes.

But there was no light in Eric's eyes now, just a bottomless, dark coldness, a void of betrayal and anguish that told her she'd been right. There could be no happy ending here.

Stay strong, she counseled herself. Stay in control. Stay focused. Think courtroom, she added. She'd handled the toughest prosecutors London and Chicago had to offer. She'd made hostile witnesses bleed.

She would not, could not, let this man break her again.

Instead she stared up at him, at those impossibly blue, impossibly demanding eyes, the hard set to his mouth and uncompromising lines of his body, and realized that while she'd made love with him just the night before, given him her heart and her soul and her body, she now faced a stranger. A very tall, very angry stranger.

"I—I didn't know what else to do," she said honestly.

His mouth twisted. "The truth would have been a good start."

Something deep inside snapped. "The truth?" she asked, shoving back from him. "The truth?" Oh, she could give him the truth, all right. Had lived with the truth for ten years. "The truth was that we were together that night out of sorrow, not love. The truth was that you turned to me in need," she said raggedly, "because I was the only one there." He'd been blind with grief, she too crazy in love to turn away from him. And while it had been her choice, the memory and the aftermath had never quit slicing her up inside.

"You say you loved me, and maybe you did, but not the way I loved you. I knew it was wrong and I knew it wasn't returned, but that didn't staunch the flow. I stood there that morning wrapped in a sheet and shivering, able to smell you, feel you inside me still, while you kissed me on the forehead and told me I was a good friend, then walked out the door without turning back. You might as well have patted me on the head as if I was the golden retriever you'd grown up with. I couldn't breathe, Eric. I wanted to die.''

His gaze darkened. "Leigh—"

"I was at your dad's funeral, did you know that? No, of course you didn't, and that's okay, but I was there, Eric, bleeding for you and wanting to give you my support, even when you didn't know.''

"You should have told me.''

"Told you what? Told you when? When you called me and said you weren't coming back, that your life was in Cloverdale with your mom and Becky? That you were sorry you made love to me and would I please just go to Oxford?''

He pinched the bridge of his nose. "That's not fair.''

"Life isn't. I learned that the hard way.''

"Damn it, Leigh, I had no idea you were pregnant.''

Would it have made a difference? some place deep inside her longed to ask, but she refused to let the question past the wedge of hot emotion in her throat. The answer didn't matter.

For years she dreamed of marrying Eric. For years she dreamed of creating a family of their own. But as she looked at the contempt in his eyes, the hard lines of his face, she realized no matter how badly she still longed for that family, Connor deserved better than living in a house where his father could barely stand the sight of his mother.

"I didn't want your pity then, Eric, and I don't want it now.''

"Pity?" he practically growled. "Is that what you think this is about?"

There was no thinking about it. "I know you, Eric," she said with a brittle smile. The little boy who'd been abandoned by his birth parents had grown into a man determined never to let down anyone he deemed to be in his care. Not his mother, not Becky and not, if he'd known she was pregnant, Leigh. "I know your sense of right and wrong. If I'd told you about the baby, you would have added my pregnancy to your shoulders like another burden and silently trudged on. You might have even asked me to marry you out of some misplaced sense of responsibility."

"Misplaced sense of responsibility? We're talking about my child!"

Later, she knew. Later she would fall apart. Now she had to remain strong. "And I'm talking about forever, Eric. I'm talking about a child who deserves better than to grow up in a family where his parents married only to compensate for a mistake." She hesitated briefly before plunging on. The truth, she reminded herself. He wanted the truth.

"I grew up like that," she reminded. "I grew up the child of parents who married simply because of one careless night. And I watched my mother and father come to hate each other. They couldn't look at each other, couldn't say a word, without the anger and resentment boiling through." And she'd always known it was her fault, her fault her parents hated each other, her fault her mother had lived a life without the love of a good man.

Now she felt her composure slip, the emotion she'd been fighting buck up against decisions made a lifetime ago. "I would have done anything," she said, "anything to spare my child, spare you, that same agony."

Eric stepped toward her. "I'm not your father."

"No, you're not, and I know that. But I also know marriages based on the wrong reasons never last. And I wanted better than that. I wanted more than the illusion of a family."

Eric squeezed his eyes shut, opened them a moment later. "Christ."

The clamp around her heart tightened, making breathing impossible. "We can't change the past," she said quietly.

Outside the sun was just about gone, leaving shadows to spill into the foyer. "No," Eric said, "but you sure as hell changed the future." Then he turned and walked toward the door.

Leigh sucked in a sharp breath, surprised by how jaggedly it scraped. "Where are you going?"

He turned back to her, frowning. "I can't be with you right now," he said in a voice devoid of all emotion. "I can't look at you. I don't even know who you are."

And then he walked away.

One moment, one decision, one mistake.

Leigh moved woodenly to the open door and watched him slide into his car, but she refused to go after him. There was nothing else to say. They had only the truth now, and as she'd always, always known it would, it destroyed everything.

His black Jeep roared to life, with Eric checking the sidewalk before backing out the driveway. She watched his taillights fade into the darkness, amazed that she could stand there so silently, so still, while her heart quietly and violently shattered.

* * *

Jake stared out over the twinkling lights of downtown Chicago. "She doesn't understand, Gretchen. She says I'm breaking her heart. How do I fight that?"

Through the scratchy international phone line, his sister sighed. "She's still pressuring you to go back to Texas?"

"She's tired of the cloak-and-dagger routine, she says. Tired of not knowing where I am. Tired of sleeping alone."

"Can you blame her?"

"No," Jake admitted. "But I can't change anything. Not now." Not until he found his brothers and sisters and helped stamp out the danger threatening them all. He'd done everything he could to help Tara through this. He called her every night. He sent her flowers. He'd even hired bodyguards to make sure she stayed safe. The thought of someone nabbing her—or his parents—to use as a pawn against him turned his blood to ice. Of course, Tara had no idea that the nice couple who'd moved in next to her were really a former Green Beret and a martial arts expert, but for now he figured the less she knew, the better. If she knew more, she'd demand explanations.

Explanations were one commodity he did not have to offer.

"Hang in there," Gretchen advised. "Are you any closer to clearing your friend's name?"

"Maybe," he said. "A few leads look promising. We should have a second evaluation on his computer within a day or two."

"You don't think…"

"No." He didn't need her to finish the question. "He's not one of us." The thought, the possibility that his friend was really his brother had kept Jake awake night after night. Both men were tall and excelled with numbers, but when Jake looked at Eric, he didn't feel that distorted buzz he'd felt with Marcus and Gretchen. And even when he'd probed his friend, there'd been no mention of strange dreams or fractured memories. No mention of a dark-haired woman with kind blue eyes or a big bear of a man who wore thick glasses. No memory of the elegant old house or the beach.

Even Marcus had those memories.

Plus, if Eric Jones was really one of the Proteans, as the press so loved calling them, that meant he could be behind the World Bank heist. And that Jake couldn't believe. "When the evidence comes in, we'll know for sure, but I don't think so."

"I'm sorry," Gretchen said softly.

He turned from the dazzling parade of lights streaming down Lake Michigan and stared at the muted television screen, where the Cubs and the Mets were locked in a surprising pitchers' duel. "We'll find the others, Gretchen. I'm sure of it."

"Marcus told me he dreamed of her last night... dreamed of Mother."

That snagged Jake's attention, brought a quick stab of grief. He'd lost his mother before ever really knowing her. But he had his siblings. Marcus and Samantha had traveled to Gretchen and Kurt's safe house on the nearly deserted island of Brunhia, where they were now planning their wedding. "The same dream or something new?"

"Her singing 'Twinkle Twinkle Little Star.'"

Jake smiled. "I like that dream."

"He doesn't remember the toys, though. Maybe he was too young."

"Probably." But Jake remembered. Boxes and boxes of fantastical toys, toys he'd never seen in a store or catalog. Robotic dogs capable of carrying on conversations, puzzles that changed shape and size as you worked them.

"How are the disks coming?" His gut insisted the answers to so many mysteries were contained in the sophisticated code Henry Bloomfield—*his father*—had devised to protect them all. If the truth fell into the wrong hands, the consequences could be catastrophic. "Any progress?"

"More every day. By the time you get here we should be close."

Jake frowned. He wanted to be on the island with his sister and brother, be there when the code was broken, but he couldn't leave Chicago. Not yet.

"Just a few more days," he promised Gretchen, much as he'd promised Tara. She'd be traveling with him, the first real quality time they'd spend together in months. Of course, the fact that they'd be traveling to Brunhia for Marcus and Samantha's wedding when their own was on indefinite hold hadn't exactly gone over well.

Instinct warned that the tension brewing between the two of them was about to hit a full rolling boil.

"That's fantastic news, Glenn. Tomorrow morning?"

"I'm pretty sure."

"Wonderful." Leigh hung up the phone a few minutes later and picked up her coffee mug, indulged in a long sip. The jolt of caffeine swam through her, punched deep. Optimism welled.

Tomorrow. By this time tomorrow morning, one of the two private investigators she'd hired, Glenn Moore, promised to arrive with a key piece of evidence to clear Eric's name. The second investigator, Alice Brady, had checked in the afternoon before, announcing that she, too, had stumbled across some very "interesting" information.

Please, Leigh thought, staring out the window toward her backyard. Please let this nightmare be almost over. Then she frowned. Resolving the case would not end the nightmare, not now that the truth had spilled into the open, gouging out the distance between her and Eric more firmly, more permanently, more deeply than time or an ocean ever had. She'd seen the look in his eyes, the hot, glinting light of betrayal.

I can't be with you right now. I can't look at you. I don't even know who you are.

Long, sleepless hours later, the words still twisted her up inside. She'd dedicated her career to defending others, but could find no defense for herself. She'd tried to explain, to make him understand, but knew some things could never be forgiven. Keeping a man's child from him was one of them.

The doorbell jarred her. She jumped, knocking over the coffee as she swung toward the front door. Connor had gone to a friend's house after church. She'd come home and made phone calls, and hadn't yet changed clothes.

She wasn't expecting anyone.

Through the curtains in the living room she saw the Jeep. Through the peephole, the man. The anger. He dominated her doorstep just as he'd always dominated her heart, a tall man with piercing blue eyes. Every instinct she had for self preservation demanded that she turn and walk away, but she'd never been a coward.

"Eric," she said, pulling open the door. Her pulse staggered and her breathing hitched, but she kept her voice steady. The attorney's voice. "I didn't expect you today."

His lips curled in a gesture far more similar to a snarl than a smile. "I don't run from my problems, Leigh."

She swallowed. "I never said you did."

"I don't tuck tail and hide, either. I don't pretend."

As she had. He didn't say the words, but they echoed through the foyer, her heart, loud and clear. "I did what I thought best."

The planes of his face hardened. "And I'm doing what I think is best. I'm meeting with two attorneys tomorrow, one to take over the case and the other to draw up formal custody papers."

The words, cold and emotionless, slammed into Leigh like a wrecking ball. She reached numbly for the antique hall tree, but could do nothing to disguise the sharp intake of air. "That's not the answer, Eric."

"I need someone I can trust to represent me," he bit out. "And I'm not going to miss another day with my son."

Leigh stared blindly at the man standing before her, the man she'd made love with, made a child with. But as had happened the night before, she saw only a stranger, an angry, betrayed man who threatened every aspect of the life she'd built for herself and her son. "I would never keep him from you," she said quietly.

"What would you call the past ten years?" he asked, then abruptly lifted a hand. "No, never mind. The past doesn't matter. It's the future I'm interested in, the future I want."

The future. A new lawyer to represent him. And his son. But not her. "Do you really think I'd let my son's father go to prison?"

"I've already told you, Leigh. I don't know what you'd do, not anymore."

He looked tired, she noted. As wrung out as she felt.

She doubted he'd found much sleep the night before, either. "Do what you have to, Eric, but know I'm going to do what I have to, as well."

His eyes narrowed. "What the hell is that supposed to mean?"

She lifted her chin, let a fire of her own flash in her eyes. She deserved his anger, deserved his contempt, but she would not let him bully her, and she would not beg. She hadn't set out to hurt him.

"Contrary to what you think," she said, "I don't run and hide, either. I don't pretend. And I don't quit."

And by God, she was not letting this man go to prison.

"I'm not asking you to quit, Leigh. I'm telling you what's going to happen."

She curled her fingers around the edge of the hall tree. "What do you expect me to say? Okay? Fine? Whatever you say?"

His mouth twisted. "Hardly."

"Then go," she said abruptly. Her heart broke on the words, but she forced the attorney to remain in place, refused to let the woman bleed through. "If you're not here to have a discussion, if you're not ready to listen, then turn and walk out the door."

Eric held her gaze long and hard, then swore under his breath. Then he did exactly as she asked. He turned and walked out the door down the winding walkway, didn't look back.

Leigh watched him go, waited until the door thundered shut behind him. Then she uncurled her bloodless fingers and strode to the bay window in the living room. The sky was a brilliant blue, a scattering of fluffy white clouds dotting the horizon.

The truth shone as brightly as the early afternoon sun.

The past was gone, but the future remained, and Leigh

would fight for that with everything she had. Eric Jones could fire her, he could walk out the door without looking back, but he could not, would not, stop her.

Despite the lies and the heartbreak that stood between them, she loved him far too much to turn her back on him now.

Connor ran back on a sharp line drive straight up the center, caught it on a bounce, then spun around and fired the ball toward first half a step before the runner hit the base.

Eric surged to his feet and let out a low whistle. "Good throw, Connor!" The boy flashed a smile toward the bleachers, then hunkered down into a ready stance to await the next pitch.

Pride beamed through Eric as bright and warm as the late-afternoon sun bearing down from a cloudless sky. He'd arrived at the ballpark shortly before the first pitch, having driven in circles before losing the news vans tailing him. Connor had seen him the second he'd walked toward the bleachers, breaking away from his team to run over and grin up at Eric.

"You made it!" he'd said, his wide smile revealing the dimple he shared with his father. "This is so cool!"

Eric's throat had tightened. "I wouldn't have missed it for the world."

And he wouldn't have. He'd already missed so much, his birth, his first words, seeing those first tentative steps, teaching his son to ride a bicycle and throw a baseball.

Leigh had done a good job with him. Eric had to admit that, even as betrayal again slashed through him. For a while, during the long dark hours of the night when he'd stood on his patio overlooking the quiet streets of Lincoln Park, numbness had replaced the sharp edges of shock. But the second he'd seen her standing in the sunny foyer and wearing a soft, feminine sundress at complete odds with the cool defiance in her eyes, the roaring had started all over again, an incessant drumming in his blood, a raw bleeding deep inside he didn't know how to stop.

He had a son, damn it. He and Leigh. They'd created a child. If that night had been a cheap one-night stand, a drunken slapping of bodies in the dark, then maybe he could understand her silence. But it hadn't been. He'd been blind with grief that night, and Leigh had been there. Leigh. His friend. His *best* friend. They'd shared laughter and secrets, good times and bad. She'd confided in him about her lonely childhood, when she'd felt responsible for her parent's lousy marriage. And in turn, he'd told her about the happy years with the Joneses, but the relentless curiosity, as well, about the man and woman who'd given him life, then abandoned him.

Another crack of the bat sent a ball soaring over Connor's head. He raced back, but the ball fell toward the centerfielder, who made a solid diving catch. Connor whooped and ran toward his friend, high-fiving the third out of the inning.

Eric stood and clapped, watched his boy run to the dugout, sparing a quick grin for his father. Staggered, Eric sat down, wondering how it could be so damn easy. Wondering how ten years could stand between them, but with a simple smile, all they'd lost faded to the background, replaced by the promise of what lay ahead.

He wanted that future, damn it.

He saw her then, Leigh, walking toward him. She no longer wore the simple sundress, but khaki shorts and a red scoop-neck T-shirt, her hair in a sporty ponytail like so many of the other mothers. Her gaze was riveted on Eric. "You came."

"I promised him I would."

He heard the sharp intake of breath, watched her glance toward the dugout.

"He's good," Eric said.

Her smile was sudden and blinding, and it damn near stopped his heart. "He's the best."

That, Eric thought, they could agree on.

"How much did I miss?"

He bit back words that didn't need to be said. "Only two innings."

She started to turn away then, in search of another seat, but Eric reached for her hand. "He'll want to see us together."

Apprehension lit Leigh's eyes, a pain he didn't want to see. "Isn't that a farce?"

He tugged her down beside him, ignoring the aroma of apples that came with her, an aroma that still clung to the sheets of his bed. "Some farces are worth the price."

The image of father and son, side by side and laughing, stayed with Leigh through the quiet hours of the night, accompanying her to the office the following morning. The remaining innings of the baseball game had passed quickly, with Connor making spectacular play after spectacular play. She'd watched him run and dive for balls, spin and throw, swing the bat, and after each, he'd turned and beamed a smile at them. His parents. Seated side by side, thigh to thigh.

It had been like one of those fractured dreams, the kind that brought waves of pleasure and shards of pain.

Afterward he'd run up to them grinning, a baseball

hat hiding his scraggly hair and grass stains at the knees of his pants, and suggested pizza. One look into his hopeful smile, and Leigh knew there was no way she could deny his request.

Father and son shared more than blood. She'd sat across from the two of them, barely able to quit staring at the twin sets of piercing blue eyes, the twin dimples, the twin smiles. They both loved sausage and mushroom pizza, root beer and Jimmy Buffet.

For a few hours they'd almost been like a family.

Some farces are worth the price.

Others broke hearts.

She'd known the risk, the gamble, from the moment Eric had walked into her office that unbearably hot morning a week before. She'd known, but with three simple words spoken in that deep, achingly familiar voice, she'd thrown every shred of caution out the fifty-seventh floor window.

I need you.

She was still sitting there, staring at the coffee long since cold, when the intercom buzzed ten minutes later.

"There are two gentlemen here to see you," Julia announced. "Glenn Moore and Seth Mitchell."

Leigh's heart hitched painfully, then started to pound a frenetic rhythm. She'd put the wheels in motion, hoping for just this outcome. But now that the moment of truth lay at hand, apprehension bled through.

One moment. One decision. One mistake.

Please, she thought, rising to go greet her visitors. *Please don't let this be another mistake.*

Forty-five minutes later, she sucked in a sharp breath and pressed the buzzer to the outer door of Eric's brownstone. Her pulse raced crazily as the seconds ticked by.

And then Eric opened the door.

* * *

He paced the length of his elegant hotel room, dreading the phone call he had to return. He didn't know how his superior had learned the damning information, how news he'd tried to squelch had screamed across the country with damning speed.

Close, damn it. He was so close. Just three more deposits into his bank account and he'd be set for life.

He should just leave. He should get on the next plane to nowhere and lose himself in a faraway land, among a throng of nameless, faceless people.

But there was no escaping those after Jake Ingram. Their reach was far and deadly. They would never give up, never quit looking for Bloomfield's secrets, secrets they believed Ingram could and would lead them to. He knew that. His only option was to correct his mistake.

"She's become a liability we can't afford," came the hard, condemning voice seconds later. "She knows too much."

"She can't prove his innocence," he protested. Yes, he knew about the meeting she'd had at her office, the shocking discovery she'd made, but that didn't mean she would uncover the full truth. One puzzle piece did not a picture make. "The cards are stacked too high against him. The evidence is ironclad and compelling."

"Jones's laptop has vanished from the lab in Quantico. Did you know that?"

A brutal sliver of cold cut straight through him. "That's impossible."

"I've already had to take corrective measures there." A pause, then a hard sound of displeasure. "Do I need to intervene in Chicago, too?"

"No." Absolutely not. He'd seen what intervention

entailed. He'd attended the funeral. "I have the situation under control."

"Stop her," his superior barked. "Stop her before she stops you."

The line went dead, but the threat reverberated through the spacious, elegantly decorated room. And for one of the few times in his life, unease quickened through him. He'd made a rare mistake. He'd underestimated the leggy brunette. He'd underestimated her tenacity, the strength of her bond to the man who stood accused.

The man who *had* to take the fall.

And for his mistake, there had to be a price. A consequence.

But he wouldn't be the one to pay.

Twelve

She was the last person Eric expected to see. He wouldn't let himself think about what he wanted. The shorts and T-shirt of the day before were gone, as was the ponytail, replaced by a severely tailored pantsuit, this one black and sexy as hell, despite its conservative cut. She looked tired, her face pale, dark shadows smeared beneath her eyes.

The blast of compassion caught him by surprise, the sudden, blinding desire to crush her in his arms and never let her go. Leigh. The girl he'd left behind, the woman she'd become, the mother of his son.

And that made him angry all over again, not at her, but this time at himself.

"Leigh."

She lifted her chin. "Eric. I'm glad you're here."

Just two days ago, her words would have lit through him. He would have drawn her to him and tasted her mouth, suggested they go upstairs. Now he just looked at her. He didn't trust himself to move, to speak.

"There's been a development," she said, and though her voice rang strong and true, a sheen of moisture glazed her eyes. And her hands, he noted raggedly, were trembling. Poised, graceful, refined Leigh's hands were trembling. "I have information you and your new attorney will be interested in." She rummaged around inside a large leather satchel slung over her shoulder, then handed him a shoebox.

Every instinct he had went on red alert. "What's this?"

"Letters," she answered simply, then swung the killing blow. "From your birth mother to your birth father."

Eric just stared. First at Leigh, then at the box in his hands. "What are you talking about?"

"Your new lawyer might be interested in them," she said in a curiously neutral voice. "You're not a Protean, Eric. Far from it. You were conceived the old-fashioned way. In love."

Confusion swirled fast, sucked deep. Questions hammered hard. "My birth parents?"

A warm smile curved her lips. "There's someone you need to meet." In one smooth move, she stepped aside and gestured down the steps of his brownstone to where a tall graying man with piercing eyes stood watching.

Recognition hit hard and fast, followed quickly by shards of denial.

But then the man moved toward him, and Eric found himself staggering down the steps. The man moved haltingly, each step appearing painful and cautious. He looked weathered, as if life had beaten him down as violently as a thunderstorm tearing through a field of wheat. His clothes were simple, faded blue jeans and a thin plaid shirt. But his face…the eyes and the mouth, the line of his jaw…

It was like looking into a foggy mirror of time and space.

The older man glanced nervously behind Eric, toward Leigh, then stopped and stuck out his hand. "Hello, son."

Eric just stared. Shock ground through him. Blood

pounded hard. In the street beyond, cars ambled by, but he couldn't look away from the older man, couldn't stop the world from spinning. "My father died ten years ago."

The older man lifted a shaking hand to Eric's face. "Sweet mercy, you have your mother's cheekbones."

The words sent Eric reeling. He staggered back from the man, his touch, his words. "Who the hell are you?" he demanded.

The man didn't follow, just gazed at Eric through tired blue eyes awash with awe. "Seth," he said in a roughened voice. "Seth Mitchell."

"Your birth father," Leigh said from behind him.

Eric spun toward her, felt the questions burn through him. "Birth father?" All that control he prided himself on and relied on crumbled. "My birth mother and father gave me up for adoption thirty-three years ago and never looked back."

"Your mother died," the man said quietly. "In a car accident. She was twenty years old."

The words slammed into Eric. Denial rushed through wounds he'd worked damn hard to numb. "That's not true." Couldn't be. "She brought me to an orphanage, said she couldn't deal with me anymore."

"No," Seth said, motioning to the shoebox Eric had dropped somewhere along the way. "Your mama would never have given you up. She loved you with every corner of her heart."

Eric glanced down at the box, the letters spilling out. Faded envelopes addressed to a man named Seth Mitchell, from a woman named Tammy Adams. Letters without stamps, never mailed.

Tears glistened in the man's blue, blue eyes, eyes so like Eric's. So like Connor's. "I was in Vietnam," Seth said in a voice that could only be described as broken. "Got drafted straight out of high school. Tammy didn't know she was pregnant when I left."

The man's words came at Eric through a long, foggy tunnel. Seth, he said his name was. Seth *Mitchell.* Eric's own middle name. "How long were you there?"

"Six years," Seth answered slowly, rubbing a hand absently over his shoulder. "I would have left that hellhole sooner, but after Tammy died, there didn't seem much point."

Emotion careened through Eric, hard and fast and brutal. "A child wasn't important enough to come home to?"

A sound broke from Seth's throat, so low and anguished it barely sounded human. "I never knew about you," he rasped. "Tammy never told me, except in those letters, which she never mailed. She said knowing would have made it harder on me, and she didn't want that." The tears did more than glint in his reddened eyes now, they spilled over. "And then, after the accident, my cousin sent me an article from the newspaper, saying Tammy Adams and her two-year-old son had been killed when a truck blew a tire and jumped the guardrail...."

His words trailed off, but not the grief carved into every line of his face.

"That's why he didn't come home," Leigh said, lifting a hand to Eric's arm. "He thought you were dead."

Nothing prepared Eric. Nothing could have. All these years he'd lived with the cold knowledge that his parents had decided they'd rather live without him. That they'd taken him to an orphanage, then turned and walked away without looking back. He'd never looked for them, never attempted to find out who they were. Never wanted to.

Or, at least, he'd never allowed himself to want to.

But now he stared at this tall, whipcord-lean middle-aged man named Seth Mitchell, a man who shared his eyes and his jaw line and his dimple, a man with sorrow etched in his face and love shining in his gaze, who claimed to be his father.

And God, how he wanted.

"I don't understand," he said, turning to Leigh. Anything, anything to break the emotions swamping him, emotions he didn't come close to knowing how to handle.

Tears glistened in her eyes. "I wanted to prove you weren't a Protean," she said. "I thought if I could prove you were conceived the old-fashioned way, not in a laboratory, then we'd dismantle one prong of the prosecution's case."

His new attorney had said the same thing. "You should have told me," he ground out. Prepared him. "You should have told me what you were trying to do."

"And get your hopes up?" The warm breeze whipped at a few loose strands of hair, prompting her to slide them behind her ear. "I didn't know what we'd find, Eric, if anything. It could have been a wild goose chase."

"Are you...are you sure?" he asked, and hated the way his voice broke on the question. Hated the way he wanted.

"You have a birthmark on your lower back," Seth said in a quiet voice. "Tammy told me about it in the letters. You have a cowlick at the back of your part," he continued. "So do I."

So did Connor.

"The stories match up," Leigh put in. "My P.I. visited religious-affiliated orphanages in Iowa, looking for information about a two-year-old boy surrendered around 1970. In a small town outside Cedar Rapids he found a woman whose mother used to run an orphanage. The woman had been a child at the time, and she'd played with the kids. She remembered a little boy with the bluest eyes in the world, a little boy who'd been dropped off at the orphanage by a middle-aged woman who claimed the boy's mother had died in a car accident, leaving no one to care for him. The woman ran off without completing the paperwork.''

"Dottie never approved of me," Seth bit out. "She was a big part of the reason Tammy and I didn't get married before I left for 'Nam.''

"From there it was fairly simple," Leigh explained. "Glenn, my P.I., searched newspapers for information about young women killed in car accidents that spring and quickly stumbled across Tammy Adams. Her aunt—your great-aunt—still lives in Pella, which is where you were born. She told Glenn that her niece Tammy and her young son, Eric Mitchell, had died in a tragic car accident, and that her sister, Dottie, had never been the same.''

Eric swore softly.

"If I'd known," Seth put in, curling his hand around Eric's forearm. "If I'd had any idea you were still out there, alive somewhere, I would moved heaven and earth to find you.''

Slowly, Eric looked up and met Seth's gaze. His own gaze, his father's gaze. "We'll need a DNA test.''

"Already arranged," Leigh said in a brisk, efficient manner. "You have an appointment this afternoon.''

"Read the letters, son," Seth added. "Tammy's aunt found them in her sister's attic after Dottie died and brought them to me. It was like having you and your mama back. She wrote down everything, what she felt when she found out she was pregnant, how badly she wanted to tell me, but why she'd decided it was for the best if she didn't, when she first felt you kick, when she gave birth. Your first smile and laugh. Your first word.''

"What was it?'' Eric asked abruptly.

Seth laughed. It was a warm sound, solid and sustaining. "Cookie.''

Eric felt the smile start in his heart, slide to his mouth.

"Dada was second,'' Seth added. "Mama was third.''

"Dada,'' Eric repeated quietly. Incredulity wound deep. A week ago he'd been a man living alone. Two days ago he discovered he had a son. And now, if Leigh and the deep hammering of his heart were right, he had a father. "Dad.''

Seth Mitchell smiled. "Eric,'' he said in that tired, hoarse voice of his, then pulled him into his arms. "Son.''

He looks like you, Seth. I wish you were here with us now. I wish you could see your boy. I wish you could hold him. He brings unbelievable joy to my heart, even when he wakes up hungry at four in the morning. Those are some of the most special times, when I'm sitting in the dark with your child at my breast, watching him suckle and knowing no matter how many miles separate us, no matter how much time stands between us, a part of you will always be with me.

Not telling you is the hardest thing I've ever done. I hope you forgive me when you get back. You need to know I did it out of love, nothing else. I know how hard it is for you being there in that hellhole so far away from home. And that's why I've kept news of your son from you. If you knew, it would make every day more of an agony for you, and I love you too much for that. I love you too much to add to the burden you carry. You're doing a noble thing there in that land so far away from ours, fighting a war that has nothing to do with us.

Know that I think about that all the time, of how proud I am of you. And I pray. God, how I pray. I pray you'll come home safe and sound to me. I pray I'll see you teaching our son how to throw a baseball or ride a bike. I pray you'll forgive me. I pray you'll always, always remember how very much I love you.

Seth had remembered, Eric thought, putting down his mother's yellowed letter and swallowing against the rock of emotion jammed in his throat. He'd remembered, and he'd never stopped loving her back. Never stopped mourning her. He'd returned safe and sound from Vietnam, as she'd begged him to do, as he'd promised to do, but he had no home to return to. No fiancée. No child. Only memories, shadows of the past, echoes of all that would never be.

Eric and Seth had submitted samples for a DNA test early in the afternoon, but now, as Eric stood on his patio and watched the darkening summer sky, he knew he didn't need those test results. Seth Mitchell was his father. He knew that deep in his bones, just as he'd known Connor was his son the second he'd laid eyes on the boy. He had a father, he thought again. And a son.

And he owed both to Leigh.

God, Leigh.

"Think about her for a change," Jake had bit out just that morning. He'd stopped by to let Eric know Ethan was expecting lab results on Eric's laptop by early the next morning. He'd known something was wrong the second he'd walked in the door, and Eric had seen no reason not to tell him about Connor.

It hadn't taken long to realize Jake already knew. The quick rush of betrayal had been like a blow to the gut.

His friend had shoved a hand through his hair and sworn softly. He'd also taken her side. "She was twenty years old and so crazy in love with you she could barely see straight," he'd all but growled.

Eric hadn't wanted to hear that. "We were friends."

Jake let out a harsh laugh. "Only in your eyes, Indy. The rest of us saw it plain as day."

"That doesn't change the fact that she lied to me."

"She never lied to you."

"She kept my son from me."

Jake's mouth twisted. "A son she had no way of knowing you would want. You were marrying Becky. You encouraged Leigh to go to Oxford. She loved you. After her train wreck of a childhood, you really think she would thrust an unwanted child on you? Ruin your plans? Take away the life she thought you wanted? Right or wrong, she loved you far too much for that."

Love. The word stabbed deep.

"I never thought I'd say this to you, Indy," Jake had said as he'd left. "But you're a goddamn fool."

She had a party to plan. Leigh stepped off the elevator with her briefcase in one hand and a tall cup of coffee in the other, deep in thought about Connor's approaching birthday. She could invite his baseball team, take them out for paintball and pizza.

She'd have to invite Eric.

Her heart stumbled on the thought. *Eric.* He would be part of their lives from this day forward; nothing could change that. She certainly wouldn't try. Father and son deserved to get to know each other, develop a relationship. Both fathers and both sons.

The sight of Eric standing on the sidewalk yesterday beneath the glare of the late-morning sun and staring at Seth Mitchell, just staring, would stay coiled around her heart forever.

"You've had several calls already," Julia said as Leigh headed to her office. "I put them in voice mail."

"Thanks," she said absently. "You're a gem."

"Leigh?"

She paused, turning to look at her friend's concerned face. Before Eric walked back into her life, the two had often shared lunch, secrets, laughter. "Something wrong?"

"I was going to ask you that," Julia said. "You don't look like yourself."

She forced a smile. "Just tired, I suppose."

"The Jones case?"

Her heart kicked, hard. "You could say so."

"Maybe the calls will be good news, then," Julia said. "Someone named Ethan Williams called a little while ago, said he had something important to tell you."

Adrenaline mixed with caffeine to send Leigh's pulse racing. Ethan. The computer. "Thanks," she said, heading down the hall.

After unlocking the door to her office, she strode in and found the red light blinking on her phone console. She set down her briefcase and her coffee and quickly reached for the receiver, but a single sheet of white paper snagged her attention and stopped her cold.

YOU WERE WARNED...

The letters were large and bold and black, and they appeared traced from a stencil kit.

Leigh sucked in a jagged breath, but the room kept spinning. "Julia?" she asked, pressing the intercom buzzer. "Has anyone been in my office this morning?"

"Not that I'm aware of. Something wrong?"

"Maybe," she said. "Just to be sure, why don't you call security for me, ask them to come up immediately."

The red light kept blinking, prompting her to shift her attention to the calls, rather than the notes. She picked up the receiver, hating the way her hands shook. She wasn't a woman to be afraid. She didn't jump at shadows. And yet, she couldn't banish the coldness drilling through her, the chilling awareness that they'd reached the final act.

"Someone's mighty interested in hearing what you have to say," Bob Kitchens, chief of security, said fifteen minutes later. He held the tweezers up so Leigh could see the small device pinched between the prongs, a round metallic disc that looked like a hearing aid.

Her heart rate quickened. "Someone bugged my office?"

"Looks like it."

The implications horrified her. "Are there others?"

Bob dropped the device into a plastic bag. "We'll do a sweep and get the police up here, but for now, I'd recommend you make private calls elsewhere."

Leigh brought a hand to her face and pressed two fingers against her temple. Her mind raced to recall the conversations she'd had from her office phone, conversations that would have revealed the defense strategy she was building.

"Clean as a whistle," Ethan pronounced a short time later, when she returned his call from the conference room. Bob had checked for bugs before she'd touched the phone. "Someone planted a damn sophisticated echo trail on the hard drive, but my friends at Quantico have confirmed the source files couldn't have originated from Indy's hard drive."

Relief staggered through her, both for the news and the fact she'd made the call from a secure line. "Can this be proved?"

"Absolutely. Source code buried deep within the deleted files contains an electronic signature incapable of being produced by Indy's computer."

"How did the first analyst miss this?" Leigh wanted to know.

Ethan let out a low, mistrustful sound. "I'm not sure he missed it at all."

"What does that mean?"

"The analyst has turned up missing. No one has seen him since I started asking questions."

A shiver ran through Leigh. Possibilities pierced deep. "You think he was on the take?"

"Highly possible," Ethan said. "If there's one thing I've learned, it's that not all good guys are good. You can't trust someone just because they wear white."

Leigh hung up the phone a few minutes later and thought back to the three words on the sheet of paper. You were warned.

They were getting close, she knew. Close enough to make someone nervous. Very nervous.

Hack confirmed that.

He'd spent the past forty-eight hours holed up in a hotel room Leigh had secured for him, and there he'd determined, through whatever magic it was he wielded with computer systems, that the convoluted cyber trails that led to Eric's computer had, a few months before, led to an aeronautics company somewhere in Oregon.

On a hunch, he'd also done some snooping into another account. And there he'd found a stream of $100,000 deposits and subsequent withdrawals starting shortly after the World Bank heist.

Leigh's heart kicked hard, sending anticipation streaming through her. This was why she'd gone into law, why she'd chosen to be a defense attorney. There was nothing like the thrill of moving in on the prey. Except this time, the prey was shaping up to be bigger than she'd ever imagined.

And far more deadly.

Yes, she'd been warned. But her prey had underestimated its opponent.

It was early afternoon before she connected with her third caller, Alice Brady, the investigator she'd sent on a wild, wild goose chase. And again, more pieces crashed into place.

For three days Alice had been doing some tailing of her own. And during those three days, she'd witnessed several late-night rendezvous in dark, out-of-the way places. Covert meetings Alice had captured on film. Sometimes the one she'd watched had just talked with a man who bore a striking resemblance to General Bruno's number two—the suspected militant who'd been photographed with Eric. Once there'd been raised voices, twice a hand-off.

Leigh hung up the phone and smiled. Yes, she'd been warned. But she wasn't a coward and she didn't scare, and now the end lay in sight. Smelling victory, she had Julia connect her to Rebecca Salinger, the federal prosecutor building the case against Eric.

"We need to talk," she told Salinger. "Today."

At precisely 3:00 p.m., Leigh was heading out the door when her office phone rang. She almost ignored the call, having all the information she needed, but on impulse, she hurried back to her desk and brought the receiver to her ear. "Leigh Montgomery."

"Ms. Montgomery?" the unfamiliar male voice greeted. "This is Joe Lewis with Trilegient Security. I'm calling to inform you the panic button has been tripped at your house."

Leigh went absolutely, deadly still. Her heart staggered hard, then hammered against her ribcage. "The panic button?"

"Dispatch tried to raise someone at the house, but no one has answered. A squad car is en route."

The bottom dropped out from her world. "How long ago?"

"Less than five minutes."

"I'm on my way." Leigh ran from her office and down the hall, jabbed at the elevator call button. Dear God. *Dear God.* There was only one way to trip the panic alarm, and that was to deliberately and manually press the button. Connor knew better than to touch that button, not unless something was wrong. They'd discussed it countless times. Security wasn't a game. Crying wolf got you killed.

Killed.

Connor.

Leigh shot into the elevator the second the doors opened and pressed the button for the parking garage. School hadn't started yet. Connor was home with Trish, the college student who looked after him during the summer. Leigh had talked to them just thirty minutes before. Everything had been fine.

They hadn't planned to go anywhere.

But now the panic alarm was sounding, and no one was answering the phone. Police had been dispatched.

The elevator doors opened to the dimly lit garage, and again Leigh ran. She reached her car and slung her briefcase into the passenger's seat, then, once inside, gunned the engine and screeched out of the garage.

Eric. She'd held off calling him today, wanting to give him time alone with his father, wanting their next encounter to be when she announced the charges against him had been dropped.

With shaking hands she battled the small buttons of her mobile phone, zipped into the stream of traffic headed north and lay on her horn.

The second Eric's deep and steady voice sounded in her ear, her heart broke a little further. "Eric," she practically breathed. "Thank God."

"Leigh?" His voice was sharp. "What's wrong?"

"It's Connor." Her breaths came in short, choppy gasps. "The security company just called. The panic alarm is going off at the house."

"Is he there?"

"He was half an hour ago, didn't have plans to go anywhere."

Eric swore softly. "Try to relax, sweetheart. I'm sure it's just a false alarm."

She held on to his voice, used it to give her calm. "I received another note today," she blurted out. "It said, 'You were warned.'"

This time when Eric swore, it was neither soft nor repeatable. "I'm on my way."

"Hurry."

"Leigh," he said, his voice strong again, calm under fire. "Breathe."

She tried to, wanted to, but her lungs wouldn't cooperate. Blindly, she reached the interstate and gunned the engine, weaving frantically through traffic. Not Connor, she thought over and over. Dear God, not Connor. He was everything that was good and right. He was the greatest gift she'd ever been given. She couldn't live without—

No. She would not let herself think like that.

Everything looked so damn normal when she turned onto her street. The Baxter kids played in their front yard, the recently retired Aucoins leisurely rode bikes, the ever-helpful Mrs. Miller played with her petunias and a middle-aged man who'd recently moved in two houses down jogged along. The trees gracefully draped over the street, providing shade and creating the illusion of calm.

There was nothing calm about the cold terror stabbing through Leigh.

And then she saw it, her house. The brick structure she'd thought of as a sanctuary sat quietly at the end of the street, seemingly untouched. No police cars outside. No ambulances. And when she turned off her engine, she heard no panic alarm ringing from the rafters. The windows were dark, the front door closed.

Relief flashed hard and profound, followed by a sharp blade of fear. The authorities had already come and gone. She was too late. They'd taken Connor away—

No, she told herself again, racing from the car and running toward her house. No. Connor was fine. There'd merely been a misunderstanding. He hadn't meant to push the button.

''Connor!'' she called, surprised to find the front door unlocked. She pushed inside and ran through the foyer, willing her eyes to adjust to the sudden darkness within. ''Connor!''

"How nice of you to join me," came a low voice from just inside the family room. "I've been waiting."

She saw the gun first, glinting from the shadows, shiny and deadly and pointed straight at her heart. Then she lifted her eyes and saw the face.

Thirteen

"**Y**ou were warned," FBI Special Agent Daniel Venturi said. "You should have let Jones take the fall. The Coalition won't let anyone get in their way."

Cold horror snaked through Leigh. A setup. She'd been lured to her house, alone. The police hadn't been there, weren't coming. "Where's my son? What have you done with him?"

Venturi's smile was cutting, deliberate. And the light in his eyes could only be called maniacal. "Why, he's racing to your side, of course. Had a phone call about thirty minutes ago from a doctor at Memorial." His lips curled maliciously. "What good son wouldn't want to be by his mother's side as she fights for her life?"

"You son of a bitch!" Leigh hissed, charging the vile man. "You told him I'd been hurt."

"Only a small lie," the agent chided. "You're about to be dead."

That stopped her. She looked in shock at his gun, remembered the phone calls from that morning. Hack had found deposits to this man's account. Alice had documented incriminating meetings. "You're working for them. You're the one who set everything up."

"I've always said a woman's place is in the home," he said, sidestepping her accusation. "That way they don't poke their noses where they don't belong."

"Eric Jones is an innocent man."

"He won't be after they find your body," Venturi predicted.

His insinuation sickened her. "Don't be ridiculous. No one will believe Eric had anything to do with this."

"He fired you, Leigh. Removed you from the case. But you kept digging. Clearly you found something you couldn't let go of, something he didn't want you to find."

"I found *you.*"

"Time to say goodbye, counselor."

A blade of panic stabbed deep, but determination kept her strong. "Not here, in my son's house. I don't want him to…find me."

"Then you should have stopped when you were warned."

"Killing me won't change the truth," she vowed, stalling. "The wheels are already in motion. You're going to fall whether I fall or not."

A guttural laugh ripped from his throat. "You expect me to believe that?"

"Believe what you want to, but the case against you doesn't stop with me. Others already know."

Alarm flickered in his normally flat eyes. He'd had her office bugged, but not the conference room. "They'll be silenced, too," he hedged. "Every trail ends somewhere."

"It's too late for that," she countered. "I found your little presents in my office. All of them, your note and your listening device." She paused to breathe, plunged forward. "It's not just me anymore," she said again, watching his eyes flash, seeing him debate her words. "You can kill me, but Eric will still be standing. You're the one who's going to fall.

"We know about the payments you've been receiving

from Bruno's man. We can prove the cyber trails leading to Eric's computer were planted. We can prove they came from an aeronautics company in Oregon." Her heart hammered hard and desperate, but she forced one of her confident, courtroom smiles to break on her lips. "And we can prove your associate in Quantico falsified his analysis of Eric's computer." She paused, let her words sink in. "He's missing, you know. Is that what happens to traitors who do sloppy work?"

Venturi was shaking his head, rage swamping his body. "You're lying."

"If I'm lying, I've got a pretty accurate imagination, wouldn't you say?"

"I'm a dead man," he muttered, then lifted his eyes to Leigh's. "But I'm not going down alone."

She saw the gleam move into his eyes, the snarl curl his lips, the gun lift to her chest. Then she saw a flash of movement from behind him.

"You're making a mistake," she stalled, working hard to keep her voice, her eyes steady. Eric moved silently behind Venturi, slipping in from the kitchen with a baseball bat in his hand. Fear and hope crashed through her as Eric positioned himself and lifted his weapon. "If you talk, we can cut a deal—"

Venturi went pale. "There are no deals for dead men," he said blankly, then moved his finger to the trigger.

It all happened so horribly fast. So hideously slow. Seconds, minutes, Leigh didn't know.

"No!"

The harsh protest ripped through the foyer as Leigh dropped to the ground. The blast of a gun echoed insidiously. She waited for the hot burn of a bullet ripping through flesh, but felt only the solid weight of another slumping down on top of her.

Shock pierced deep, but not a bullet. She struggled against the body pinning her to the hard wood of her foyer. Able to turn her head, she saw the face of the man atop her. Seth Mitchell. And he was bleeding.

"You son of a bitch," Eric roared from somewhere beyond her. Sickly, Leigh eased from beneath Seth to see Eric swing the bat toward Venturi. The agent caught a blow to his side, but didn't stop, just plowed into Eric and sent the two of them crashing to the floor, the gun trapped beneath them. They rolled, knocking into the coffee table and fighting for possession of the weapon. Eric planted a firm blow to Venturi's jaw and pinned the rogue agent beneath him, but Venturi merely laughed, jamming the barrel of the gun into Eric's stomach. "Not..." he panted "...going...alone."

"No!" Leigh crawled from beneath Seth's body and grabbed the bat, which had fallen from Eric's hands. But then Eric and Venturi were rolling again, and she couldn't see which direction the gun pointed. She dragged herself to her feet and stood over them, waiting for the right angle.

Blood. There was so much of it. Not just on her hands but smeared on the men's faces. They kept going at each other, grunting and swearing, pounding each other like punching bags. Venturi was shorter than Eric, but bulkier. And he had the advantage of being a trained federal agent. Eric was just a man protecting his family. But he had determination on his side, and Leigh cringed as he took blow after blow, giving as good as he got.

The agent rolled, pinned Eric beneath him. "In-gram...won't...win."

Leigh didn't hesitate. She lifted her son's prized bat high and smashed it against the base of Venturi's skull.

The muffled sound of a gunshot sent the room spinning. A hot scream ripped from her throat as she dropped to her knees and shoved at Venturi's unmoving form, finding Eric sprawled beneath him, blood staining his shirt.

She leaned over him, wiped the blood from his face. "Eric!"

"Call police," he muttered. "Help…Dad."

Leigh swung toward Seth, who still lay unmoving. Grief clawed at her throat.

"Love you," Eric whispered, but when she turned back toward him, she found his eyes closed, his body slack.

Jake found her in the hospital cafeteria. "Leigh! I came as soon as I heard."

She turned from the coffeepot on the stainless-steel counter and moved into the circle of his arms. "Thank you."

He held her tightly, hating like hell that the nightmare his life had become had tainted her, as well. And Eric. God, he thought. Someone was going to pay, pay hard.

The call had come in shortly after five. Leigh had been frantic, barely making sense, speaking of panic alarms and gunshots, of Eric and Seth and Agent Venturi.

Venturi.

His gut clenched.

So much made sense now, a horrible twisted sense. Why Jake had not been informed of the case against Eric until the last moment, how the evidence had been manufactured. Lennox's murder.

Venturi had played them all.

Jake pulled back and gently touched Leigh's cheek, where a nasty bruise had begun to form. Fury pierced deep. "Any news?"

Emotion glimmered in her eyes, but strength and determination shone from the brown depths, as well. "Still in surgery."

"He's a fighter." They'd been through so damn much, and had just found each other. To have it end here, now, like this, so suddenly and needlessly, was crueler than cruel. "He'll make it."

Leigh's smile seemed forced, strained. "I know."

"How's Connor?"

Her smile was tired. "I finally convinced him to go home with my mother. He wanted to stay, but he was exhausted."

"He's a good kid." Jake picked up the two cups of black coffee and gestured toward the cafeteria door. "I'll carry these for you."

"Thanks," she said as he draped an arm around her. "They ran out of coffee in the surgery lobby."

They lapsed into silence as they walked down the quiet hall and waited for the elevator. Only when the doors slid closed behind them did Leigh look up and into his eyes. "What's going on, Jake? Do you know anything more?"

It was a damn simple question. Sadly, the answers were anything but. Thoughts of Lennox crowded close, angered him all over again. The man had been decent, kind, had loved his family and spoken often of his kids. "Venturi wasn't the first agent assigned to the case. A few months ago my original contact, Lennox, took a bullet allegedly meant for me."

Leigh sucked in a sharp breath. "My God."

"Now it looks as though Lennox was the target, after

all. It seems that someone—whoever the hell is messing with our lives—wanted to take Lennox out and replace him with Venturi.''

''But why?''

''That's the question,'' Jake muttered. ''He had plenty of chances to take me out, if that was the goal.'' They'd taken his brother, after all. Why not him? ''Instead he framed my best friend and tried to have me removed from the investigation.''

Leigh's gaze sharpened. ''He must have wanted something else from you, maybe something they thought you'd learned.''

''Maybe,'' Jake said. But he didn't think so. More likely they wanted what they suspected he was about to learn. The disks Gretchen had. The code Henry Bloomfield—his father—had hidden from the world.

The implications stunned him all over again. If Jake had gone to Brunhia with Venturi in tow…

He saw them the second they rounded the corner. Jake had his arm around her; she leaned into him. She looked exhausted, he noted with a tight twist to the gut. Her face was pale, her dark hair tangled, her eyes entirely too grim. And the bruise. Purple and black smeared her cheekbone.

If the bastard who'd hurt her wasn't already dead, he would have killed the man himself.

''Indy,'' Jake said, breaking away from Leigh and striding toward the rickety and torn plastic chair. ''Someone forget to tell me about a toga party?''

Eric stood. ''I'm sure we can find a turban for you, too,'' he said, referring to the bandage swathed around his head.

Jake grinned, setting down the foam cups and pulling

his friend to him for a quick clap on the back. "How you holding up?"

"I'll live," Eric said, then winced. He'd live, but his father was in surgery. Had been for hours. And Venturi was dead, gut-shot by his own hand. Eric had been struggling for possession of the gun, but the second Leigh had slammed the bat against Venturi, the agent's eyes had gone dark and he'd turned the gun on himself, ended it all.

Taking his secrets with him to the morgue.

"I'm sorry about your dad," Jake said, pulling back. "Any word?"

"Not yet." Everything inside was cold and raw, bleeding. He'd been close, damn it. So damned close. He'd had the situation under control, had told Seth to stay in the car. He'd been about to take Venturi out when his father had roared in front of Leigh. To protect her, Eric knew. Seth had been unable to see Eric standing behind Venturi, had been willing to lay down his life to save Leigh's. To save the mother of his grandson, the woman who'd kept her own child a secret, but who'd risked her life for that of her son's father. The woman who'd reunited them all in the end.

The end.

The phrase ground through him.

Leigh moved to stand beside him and put a hand to his forearm. "You should sit."

He did. "What's the hell's going on?" he asked Jake, taking Leigh's hand and not letting go. His head throbbed a painful rhythm. "Venturi made it sound personal."

A shadow crossed Jake's face. "What did he say?"

Eric looked to Leigh. The moments when he'd seen the gun pointed at her heart were sharp and etched, but everything thereafter blurred. He could see his father falling, hear his own roar. Then there'd been a desperate struggle, a gunshot, nothing at all. He'd come to in the emergency room, received treatment for a concussion. Leigh and Connor had been there, hovering close, talking of the future the three of them would share.

The family they would be.

Eric had pulled them both into his arms and held them tight.

"When I first arrived," Leigh was saying, "he was waiting with a gun. He said 'You should have let Jones take the fall. The Coalition won't let anyone get in their way.'"

Jake swore softly.

"And then, after he'd been shot, his last words were 'Ingram won't win.'"

Eric frowned. "Won't win at what?"

Jake hung his head. "That's what I'm going to find out." He looked up suddenly, eyes burning. "I'm leaving tomorrow," he said. "For Europe. I have reason to think the answers are there."

"Hey." Eric lifted a hand to Leigh's face and gently fingered the nasty bruise. "It's after midnight. Let me call you a taxi to take you home."

She lifted her head from his shoulder and yawned, glancing around the waiting area. "This is where I want to be."

"It'll be a while yet before we can see Seth."

She brought her hand to the back of his. "You, Eric. You're the one I don't want to leave alone."

Jake had left several hours before, after the doctor had emerged from surgery, tired but optimistic. Seth's prognosis was extremely good. The bullet had ripped through the right side of his chest, missing his lung by inches. They'd repaired the damage and, along the way, discovered the bullet he'd taken for Leigh had not been his first. Vaguely, Eric remembered his father rubbing his upper chest the day they'd met, as he'd talked about Vietnam. Now he could only wonder what it had been like for his father to be alone in that wretched hellhole of a country, of a war, with nothing left to live for.

He had everything to live for now. Both of them did. They all did.

"Christ," Eric swore softly. The pounding horror of it all drilled deep. The phone call from Leigh, the desperate race across town. If she hadn't called him— *Christ*. She would have walked into Venturi's trap alone, and he would have lost her again, this time forever. "When I looked through the window and saw that bastard with a gun on you—"

"Don't," Leigh said. "It's over now."

Rebecca Salinger, the prosecutor, had called shortly before ten, confirming what Leigh had insisted was inevitable. The charges against Eric were being dropped. The evidence Leigh had gathered was compelling, Venturi's suicide damning. There would be no grand jury hearing. There would be no indictment. No trial. No prison sentence. The only verdict rendered would be one of love.

Leigh's smile was slow, blinding. "You were wrongly accused," she said. "But now you're a free man. That's all that matters."

"No, it's not." He drank in the sight of her, all soft and sleepy, her dark hair tangled around her face and her clothes torn, the bruise on her cheek. "I loved you, Leigh. I've loved you for ten years."

Moisture rushed to her eyes. "And I betrayed you."

"Only after I betrayed you." He slid his hand into her hair and leaned in for a long, slow kiss. Then he pulled back. "We hurt each other." He'd been so blown away by Connor's existence, he hadn't been able to think clearly about what it had been like for Leigh, carrying the child of a man who had apologized for the night they made love. A man who had told her she was a good friend, but that he wasn't coming back. But as he'd read his mother's letters to his father, read of the intense joy and overwhelming sorrow of going through such a special time alone, he'd realized Leigh would have felt the same way.

"I'm sorry, Leigh. I'm sorry for hurting you. I only wanted what was best."

She smiled. "I know."

The shock of learning she'd concealed his child still throbbed, but he realized they'd been young and scared and had both made mistakes. And through it all, one truth remained. She was the only woman who'd ever slipped under his skin and into his heart.

"Two days ago," he said, skimming his thumb along her lower lip, "I told you I wanted my son. I wanted my future."

Her smile turned wooden. "And I told you I wouldn't stand in your way."

"There's more," he told her. "Something else I want."

Slowly, she lifted her gaze to his. "What?"

He looked deep into her eyes, not the eyes of the girl he'd left behind, but of the remarkable, poised, gutsy woman she'd become. "Not what, but who. You, Leigh. I want you."

And he always had.

She was the only woman who could make him laugh

and make him think, make him sane and make him burn. She understood him as no one else ever had.

Leigh just stared at him, looking as if he spoke a language she didn't understand. But her eyes, they understood. They were huge, no longer dark, but filled with the warmth he'd craved for a decade. "Eric—"

"I've waited ten years, Leigh. Ten years. When I walked out of my apartment that morning, when I left you standing naked and cold and wrapped in my sheets, I had every intention of coming back. I knew I loved you, that I couldn't marry Becky."

"Eric, don't—"

"I planned to break it off with her, but then I got home and found her in the hospital, alone and broken, and she'd hold my hand and cry and make me promise never to leave her the way her father had, and…"

"If you had, you wouldn't have been the man I'd fallen in love with."

"The past will always be there," he said. "And it might always hurt." He paused, stroked the hair back from her face. "But it doesn't have to steal the future. *Our* future."

The tears overflowed then, slipped down her cheeks. "You're the only man I've ever loved."

He couldn't help it. He grinned. "Even when you thought I might be a genetic freak who stole billions of dollars from the World Bank?"

Her lips twitched. "I never thought that."

But he had. Or at least, he'd wondered. Now, instead, out of the darkest hour of his life, he'd reclaimed more than just his freedom. He had a son and a father, a future full of promise and Little League games, love and laughter and the woman he loved. The woman he'd always, always loved.

Leigh.

Epilogue

Eric stood with his feet shoulder width apart, looking outrageously appealing in a pair of fitted dirt-stained baseball pants. He pulled the bat over his right shoulder and waited.

Behind and to the left of second base, the shortstop crouched in anticipation. He seemed to be saying, "Bring it on."

The pitch came, hard and remarkably fast considering it had been thrown by a ten-year-old, zooming over the heart of the plate.

Eric swung the bat in a smooth arc, wood connecting with a resounding thud to send the ball zinging to the left of the pitcher with incredible force.

The shortstop executed a perfectly timed leap and snagged the ball several feet above his head, robbing his father of a sure base hit. Steely eyed, he fired the ball toward first, where he would have thrown Eric out, had he not already secured that through his catch.

"All right!" Leigh said, jumping to her feet. She clapped for her son and laughed as Eric sent Connor a wicked grin.

The October air was crisp, welcome hints of fall having chased away the stifling, muggy heat of summer. The sun shone brightly from a cloudless azure sky, but a cool breeze kept the temperature in check.

Leigh sat on the bleachers, among other families

watching the annual father-son, end-of-season base-ball game.

"Our son is cruel," Eric said as he jogged over to join her. He had a cap down low on his head and a gleam in his eyes.

"Our son is talented," she corrected. "He's got that killer instinct."

Eric sat beside her and picked up her hand, where he fingered the shiny new ring on her left finger. "Cruel," he said again. "What's he thinking anyway? Christmas? Doesn't he realize that's two months away?"

Leigh laughed. "He's just being sentimental."

Eric scowled, angling in for a slow, lingering kiss. "Sentimental that."

Pleasure drifted through her, followed by a flare of desire. After Eric had proposed to her, they'd agreed to let Connor pick the date. He'd been thrilled, saying this was the best gift he'd ever received. So for a date, he'd picked Christmas Eve.

"I want to spend the night with you," Eric murmured as he skimmed his mouth along her jawline to nibble at her ear. "All night. Every night. I want to go to sleep with you, wake up with you."

As opposed to the stolen moments they'd been finding during lunch hours.

Heat licked through Leigh. "I want that, too," she whispered. God, how she wanted. Burned. She'd loved Eric for so long, had thought their chance for a happy ending had come and gone long ago. Had thought he could never forgive her for the choices she'd made. The pain would always be there, she knew, but she also knew they'd both chosen the future over the past.

"Not much longer," she said, thrilling to the way his

mouth moved against hers, making promises she knew he'd keep just as soon as he could.

Eric pulled back. "Even one day is too long."

And the nights... "Seth's up," she said, changing the subject before they got themselves entirely too worked up. It was, after all, their son's baseball game, and they could hardly sneak off under the bleachers for a few minutes alone.

Eric grinned, obviously seeing right through her ploy. But Seth *was* up at the plate, wielding a bat with the same ease as both Eric and Connor. He'd recovered from his bullet wound, insisting he had too much to live for to let some deranged FBI agent steal the future.

Just as the federal prosecutor had promised, all charges had been dropped, Eric's name completely cleared. The press had followed him a few more days, wanting the blockbuster story of a man wrongly accused, but once they realized the brief statement he'd released was all he was saying, they'd backed off. Even Cantrell had gone silent. No one had seen or heard a word from the slimy reporter since the day after Venturi went down.

They'd heard from Jake twice, and while he'd been vague, Leigh and Eric had gotten the distinct feeling their friend was optimistic about getting to the bottom of the World Bank heist. He'd been reinstated immediately following Venturi's suicide. They sensed something else going on, but Jake assured them all was well, that he'd be there for the wedding come hell or high water.

All the Blues Brothers had promised to be there.

The pitcher fired the ball toward the plate, missing the edges and giving Seth a perfect ball to drill. He swung hard and sent the ball flying straight up the middle. Connor made a valiant attempt to snag it, but the ball was too high and sailed over him, landing at the feet of the centerfielder.

Seth motored around first and into second, reaching the base well ahead of the throw.

Leigh watched Connor amble over and nudge his grandfather, watched Seth nudge his grandson right back.

Trash-talking knew no age boundaries.

It amazed her how readily Connor had adapted to the new men in his life, but then, he'd always longed for a father and more grandparents. Recently, he'd begun talking of a brother or a sister.

Eric slid an arm around her shoulders and urged her toward him. "Would you look at them?"

She glanced from the warm smile on his face to the field, where his father tugged on his son's cap. "I am."

Eric let out a sound of pure amazement. "Who would have thought being accused of the World Bank heist would be the second best thing that's ever happened to me?"

She'd always heard the night was darkest just before dawn, but the phrase took on new meaning now. Had Eric never been accused, their paths might not have crossed again. Especially not with such urgency. Connor's existence would have remained a secret, Seth's identity a mystery.

"And the best?" she asked, angling her face toward his.

His smile was slow, heated. "You have to ask?"

"I'm an attorney," she reminded. "Interrogating is what I do best."

He laughed. "Well, in that case, counselor, far be it from me to keep you waiting. The answer," he said as his mouth came down on hers, "is you."

One moment, Leigh thought, awed and dazzled, knowing December could never come soon enough. One decision.

A gift to last a lifetime.

One

Max did not want to move on yet. He wasn't ready to go back to the real world. It would start all over again—women breaking all the rules of decent behavior to become the next Mrs. Strong, paparazzi angling for that one shot, that one photo, that would mark them as The Guy Who Found Max, and his business associates descending on him, both those in his employ and those who wanted to buy from him or sell. His family would catch wind of his whereabouts and they'd start plucking at his nerves again in well-intentioned worry.

His jaw hurt from clenching it. Max forced himself to relax, and then it happened.

The scooter was more difficult to maneuver than the average bicycle, Honey admitted, but she could damned well do this. The trick was in remembering that the steering was a little more exaggerated. She figured that had to do with the fact that the scooter was going a good bit faster than she'd ever learned to pedal. Velocity equaled less reaction time, so a slight easing on the handlebars more or less put the frustrating little thing into a virtual U-turn.

Honey revved up the throttle a little and grinned as the wind whipped at her hair. She was just approaching the bend in the road before it straightened out and dived straight for the beach when suddenly he **was** there, her Portuguese hottie.

They both shouted in the same instant. Honey twisted the handlebars. She forgot that she didn't have to go hard left to avoid him. She forgot that a gentle drift in that direction would have done the trick. When she tore her surprised gaze from his face—and man, what a face!—Honey found herself flying headlong at a pile of white rocks.

The front tire of the scooter struck them and she figured she was going to take one hell of a spill. But she was going too fast for the scooter to simply stop with the impact. It went airborne, and she went with it.

Max heard the delicate putter of her smaller bike before he saw her, but even that didn't give him enough time to react. He came around the curve and there she was, headed dead at him. He had no choice but to spill, and to spill fast.

Max leaned his weight hard right. Then the crazy blonde veered to her left and they were still on a collision course. Except she kept going, kept turning. *What the hell?*

He had an impression of the most incredibly wild hair and a face filled with so much real and emphatic emotion that for some reason it made him ache inside. Then he was down and the gravel was shearing the skin off his arm and his thigh. His bike zoomed onward on its side, chewing up dirt and sending dust pluming. And the blonde went right over the side of the road. On the bike.

Max had explored the island enough to know that there was a ten-foot drop to the beach on that side. And the beach was as nasty as any he had ever seen in his world travels. It was craggy and rough and wild. Trees grew aslant from between boulders on the way down, angling for life-giving sun.

She was going to get herself killed.

Max forgot all about the fact that he didn't want to be recognized. He forgot that he resented the hell out of all these people landing on what he'd come to think of as *his* island. He launched his bleeding body up from the road and ran after her.

Just as he reached the top of the jumble of rocks on the roadside, he heard her laughter. *Laughter?* It was a sound like silver bells tinkling together, light and airy and genuine, and it froze him just as he was about to leap and no doubt hurt himself even more.

"What the hell are you doing down there?" he shouted. He realized that anger was making his voice vibrate.

"Hello?" she called back.

Max got a grip. "Are you hurt?"

"Hold on!"

"Hold on for *what?*"

"I'm checking to see if everything still works." That laughter came again. "I'm all right, but the scooter has seen better days."

Not only did he have a bunch of people descending on the island, but at least one of them was certifiable, Max decided.

He began making his way down the cliff with much more decorum than he had originally intended. He no longer felt particularly inclined to play Superman.

"That stands to reason," he called down to her. "Hold on, I'm on my way."

"There's no need—" she began, then she broke off. "On second thought, ouch."

"Ouch?" She *was* hurt, he thought. He moved faster. Then he reached the beach.

She was sitting on a boulder, grinning at him. Max felt something deep inside himself start to shake. He told himself it was the aftermath of adrenaline. Throw in a good dose of anger for good measure. That explained it.

But he was arrested by her face.

It hit him again, as it had when she'd gone airborne, that he'd never seen such real and unrepentant emotion in anyone's expression. As though anything life could dish out, including spills over cliffs, was just one more grand adventure for her to savor, experience and chalk up on one side of the line or the other, as a lesson or a hoot. This, Max realized, this whole disaster, seemed to be falling on the side of hoot.

She scraped her hair away from her face. She did have a nasty abrasion on her cheek, he realized. She'd be beautiful without it. Maybe that was why he sat down in the sand in front of her. Beauty should have had him hightailing it back up the cliff as soon as he knew she was basically okay. But abraded beauty didn't quite stir the same panic in him.

He'd have to think about that later. He told himself he just wanted to make sure she was all right.

"Someone ought to lock you up in a padded cell." His voice came out in a growl.

"They've tried. I keep slipping them."

Max's frown hurt his forehead. "A little contrition might be in order here."

"What for?"

"For trying to kill me."

"I wasn't trying. It just happened."

"Well, luckily we both lived." It struck him that he sounded utterly rigid and pompous, and what was that about? Then he realized that things were still shaking inside him.

He wasn't European, Honey realized. The European part was important—as far removed from her own life as she could get. She had the strong sense that she needed to change *everything* if she was going to break her virgin curse once and for all. She had to wipe away her constants, her identity, the brackets of her real life. But by the same token, he made her mouth water. Honey watched him watching her and felt a series of little jitters dance through her blood.

His body was as nice as it had looked earlier from a distance, though he had pulled on a pair of cutoffs over the boxer shorts and he wore a blue mesh tank top now that obscured that delicious chest. His black hair was wind ruffled, wild, too long. He needed a shave in the worst way, but that just made the jitters pick up speed. His eyes were the color of her father's favorite whiskey—and they got darker as she watched.

Well, Honey thought, he was building up a good case of temper. "Oh, chill out," she told him. "No harm done."

Those beautiful eyes of his bugged a little. "No harm? You've ruined that thing beyond repair!" He waved a hand at her motor scooter. "And look at me! Look at *me!*"

"Oh, I was."

To her utter surprise, that tantalizing remark got no reaction from him at all. He was on a roll. "I left half my skin up there on the road!"

"You know, it takes two to tango."

"Two to—" He broke off and started to sputter again. Cute, she thought.

"I wasn't the only scooter on that road," she reminded him. "You came at me like a bat out of hell."

"You were in the middle of the road!"

"Who was I going to hit? A seagull?"

"Me!"

"I traveled that road earlier and there wasn't another living soul on it."

"So that means all good sense and traffic regulations go right out the window? Lady, you're a danger to yourself and to mankind."

My, he was angry, Honey thought. He stood abruptly. He was *leaving* her? He was just going to walk away from her? Men never walked away from her. She fainted or shooed them off, but they didn't walk away.

Honey's jitters took on a whole new rhythm. Slower, unsure, then speeding up again. He has no idea who I am, she realized. He doesn't know I'm an Evans and he doesn't know I'm rich. He doesn't know I work at the White House or that I drive a Mercedes. He doesn't think I'm a tease, a flirt, wild and outrageous, an accident waiting to happen. He just thinks I give validation to all those dumb-blonde jokes.

She *had* to have him. He had to be the one to free her once and for all.

An offer you can't afford to refuse!

High-valued coupons for upcoming books

**A sneak peek at Harlequin's newest line—
Harlequin Flipside™**

**Send away for a hardcover by *New York Times*
bestselling author Debbie Macomber**

How can you get all this?

Buy four Harlequin or Silhouette books during
October–December 2003, fill out the form below and send
the form and four proofs of purchase (cash register receipts)
to the address below.

I accept this amazing offer!
Send me a coupon booklet:

Name (PLEASE PRINT)

Address   Apt. #

City   State/Prov.   Zip/Postal Code
                                                             098 KIN DXHT

Please send this form, along with your cash register receipts
as proofs of purchase, to:

In the U.S.:
Harlequin Coupon Booklet Offer, P.O. Box 9071, Buffalo, NY 14269-9071

In Canada:
Harlequin Coupon Booklet Offer, P.O. Box 609, Fort Erie, Ontario L2A 5X3

**Allow 4–6 weeks for delivery. Offer expires December 31, 2003.
Offer good only while quantities last.**

HARLEQUIN®
Live the emotion™

Silhouette®
Where love comes alive™

Visit us at www.eHarlequin.com

Q42003

Silhouette®
Where love comes alive™

FAMILY SECRETS

Five extraordinary siblings.
One dangerous past.
Unlimited potential.

Collect four (4) original proofs of purchase from the back pages of four (4) Family Secrets titles and receive a specialty themed free gift valued at over $20.00 U.S.!

Just complete the order form and send it, along with four (4) proofs of purchase from four (4) different Family Secrets titles to: Family Secrets, P.O. Box 9047, Buffalo, NY 14269-9047, or P.O. Box 613, Fort Erie, Ontario L2A 5X3.

Name (PLEASE PRINT)

Address _____ Apt. #

City _____ State/Prov. _____ Zip/Postal Code

Please specify which themed gift package(s)
you would like to receive:

❏ PASSION DT5N
❏ HOME AND FAMILY DT5P
❏ TENDER AND LIGHTHEARTED DT5Q

❏ Have you enclosed your proofs of purchase?

From Silhouette Books comes
an exciting NEW spin-off to *The Coltons!*

PROTECTING PEGGY

by award-winning author
Maggie Price

When FBI forensic scientist
Rory Sinclair checks into
Peggy Honeywell's inn late
one night, the sexy bachelor
finds himself smitten with the
single mother. While Rory works
undercover to solve the mystery
at a nearby children's ranch, his
feelings for Peggy grow...but
will his deception shake the
fragile foundation of their
newfound love?

Coming in December 2003.

THE COLTONS
FAMILY. PRIVILEGE. POWER.

Where love comes alive™

Three full-length novels from
#1 *New York Times* bestselling author

NORA ROBERTS

S U S P I C I O U S

This collection of Nora Roberts's finest
tales of dark passion and sexy intrigue
will have you riveted from the first page!

Includes *PARTNERS*, *THE ART OF DECEPTION*
and *NIGHT MOVES*, all of which have been
out of print for over a decade.

Available in November 2003, wherever books are sold.

Where love comes alive™